DARKWALKER 6
OTHER REALMS

This is a work of fiction.
Similarities to persons, living or dead,
are neither intended
nor should be inferred.

ISBN-13: 978-1-951522-02-5 (DarkFluidity)

ALSO BY JOHN URBANCIK

NOVELS
Sins of Blood and Stone
Breath of the Moon
Once Upon a Time in Midnight
Stale Reality
The Corpse and the Girl from Miami
DarkWalker 1: Hunting Grounds
DarkWalker 2: Inferno
DarkWalker 3: The Deep City
DarkWalker 4: Armageddon
DarkWalker 5: Ghost Stories

NOVELLAS
A Game of Colors
The Rise and Fall of Babylon (with Brian Keene)
Wings of the Butterfly
House of Shadow and Ash
Necropolis
Quicksilver
Beneath Midnight
Zombies vs. Aliens vs. Robots vs. Cowboys vs. Ninja vs. Investment
Bankers vs. Green Berets
Colette and the Tiger

COLLECTIONS
Shadows, Legends & Secrets
Sound and Vision
Tales of the Fantastic and the Phantasmagoric

NONFICTION
InkStained: On Creativity, Writing, and Art

POETRY
John the Revelator

INKSTAINS
Multiple volumes

DARKWALKER 6
OTHER REALMS

JOHN URBANCIK

CHAPTER ONE

1.

A gray twilight lingers in the desert sky. It never changes. It's been weeks or months. The shade of gray shifts, but only slightly, to lighter and darker variations. Clouds slip across the sky like dragons. The constant whistling of rain sounds like bombs dropping in the jungles of a warzone from before he was born, and not even Jack Harlow, DarkWalker, Destroyer of Hells, has gotten used to it.

He travels with a caravan across the vast gray desert. He's incognito, as few recognize the DarkWalker without the full depth of his power glowing from inside. He's not what he was, not anymore. Not since he died. Not since his ghost was scraped from the earth.

He barely remembers the lush warmth of Shangri La. It's an impossible world he can never return to. He walks now with other refugees, former ghosts who had fallen under the control of the DarkCrawler, various criminals suffering from regret and nostalgia.

Sometimes, he helps dig for water. When they find an oasis, the trees a greener shade of gray, the leaves big and broad and soaking up whatever passes for light in this place, they follow the roots to an aquifer, usually a shallow pool of water ten or twenty feet beneath the surface. The physical work exhausts him, or at least taxes him, and he sleeps better those nights. Which is to say, he sleeps more than an hour at a time.

Most nights, he lays on a blanket like everyone else, sometimes near the elephant, sometimes near the camels, sometimes off by himself—but not too far—and listens to the night. The dropping missiles that aren't. The creaking, snapping, and buzzing of insects. The whispers of other caravan hangers-on who, like himself, aren't completely sure why they're here.

"Up ahead, in the distance," the caravanner says when she's holding court around the nightly bonfire, "is a city of dreams. Roads paved with gold. Fountains of beer and wine. When we reach it, they'll put us in the best rooms, with harps and harpsichords, with dancing girls and serving boys, scalding showers to wash away the sand and grit, ice baths, and jewels enough to make your hearts go all aflutter."

"Why would they give us any of this?" someone eventually asks.

"Because we carry the silk," she answers, "and we carry the spices. We are like gods to them." She glances at Jack Harlow when she says this. "Though I should be honest. This is a hard road we travel, and not everyone will survive."

Indeed, since Jack Harlow's joined them, they've been swarmed by shadows thrice, stalked by jackals of the nearly natural and completely unnatural sort, and circled by gunners from the wastelands weighing their options and chances. And that's just weeks or months. The caravan has been making this trip for years and decades and centuries. The caravanner, hidden behind a face scarf that only ever reveals the rust of her eyes, can make this journey in her sleep.

And she does seem to sleep.

This night, Jack Harlow floats somewhere just before actual dozing. The winds are fiercer tonight but never blow cold. A storm brews to the east. If they're traveling a straight line, he assumes east lies off to his right. There's no true sunrise or sunset here, just a gradual darkening and lightening, glimmers of a moon that seems to shift its phase but never actually dance across the sky. He wonders if they travel at the moon's pace. Once upon a time, that would've been entirely possible for him. He never knew his limits; he knows now only that they've diminished.

Death does that to a person.

The caravan travels with three full-sized wagons, all locked, all swaying as the cattle drag them across the sands. One is filled with silk in its rawest forms, woven into carpets, wrapped in bolts. There are spiders, too, a half dozen of them, presumably related, who have been traveling with the caravanner far longer than she'll admit. The second contains spices in glass and ceramic jars, pepper, cloves, nutmeg, cinnamon, and things Jack Harlow would never recognize. He was not known for his culinary skills.

The third wagon is locked, bolted, tied down and wrapped up, and carries the prisoner.

The caravanner claims the prisoner has been with her for as long as there's been sand in this desert, and will remain with her until she dies, which may or may not be soon.

This night, the third wagon rocks, gently, as inside the prisoner rails and writhes and screams and struggles. The sounds barely escape the wagon, but Jack can hardly ignore them. They're familiar sounds. He can't place them.

The caravanner kneels in the sand next to him. She says, "He doesn't suffer, if that's what worries you."

She has a habit of sneaking up on a person. He believes there's two of her, or three, and that sometimes she's invisible. His ability to know what a person or being is, the trait of watchers, lingers within him, but it's far from infallible and often silent. The caravanner remains a mystery to him. "I wasn't worried," Jack says.

"And he cannot escape," the caravanner says. "It's the strongest, most vital prison ever created, meant specifically to contain him and others like him, as rare as he is." She winks. "You know what I mean, when I say *rare*, do you not?"

He understands, but doesn't need to respond.

"I admit, he's volatile today," the caravanner says. "And the surrounding desert is quiet. I know your eyes are always roaming the horizons. And they should. We are being watched. And maybe we have acquired a betrayer."

"In the caravan?"

"Don't be so surprised. We count among our number murderers and arsonists and politicians. I've lost count of how often I've been betrayed."

"You believe I will betray you?"

"I trust you," the caravanner says, "against all reason. So yes, of course you will betray me."

Jack wants to disagree with her, but before he can say anything, she says, "Some betrayals are softer, and more hurtful, than others."

"What about the others?" Jack asks.

"I've driven this caravan alone with seven wagons carrying the bones of my enemies," the caravanner says. "I'm not worried about the others."

"And who do you think is watching us?"

She shrugs. "Just be wary. There's been movement in the night, under the moon—it's a crescent now, but that by itself doesn't mean anything."

Jack changes the subject. "Where are we going?"

"We all walk our own paths. You know this by now You'll come with us as far as the next lost city, and from there you'll travel another path."

"You sound certain."

"I am."

Jack catches a glimpse of a glint on the horizon—a quick, here for only a breath, flash of moonlight reflecting off something metal.

"And now," the caravanner says, "you see what I mean. I don't think they're here for the silk, or the spice."

Which means they're here for the prisoner, or for someone in the caravan—someone, likely Jack Harlow himself. She doesn't say it, but he knows it's true. He's left a trail of enemies. The third wagon has ceased rocking and gone silent. "There's three of them," Jack says. "They've been shadowing us for seven nights. If they meant to attack, they would have."

The caravanner spends a moment looking out to the horizon. "Only three?"

"Others come and go, but go out of their way to avoid those three."

"Perhaps," the caravanner says, "we should send an envoy. What do you think?"

"Are you asking me to walk unarmed into the desert to meet three suspicious strangers, who may or may not be shadows, and who may or may not have our best interests at heart, if they even have hearts, to announce our intention to continue traveling through the desert?"

She smiled. "We might just continue traveling, and thus make our intentions known." She rises to her feet, brushing sand off her knee, and says, "You are indeed wise, traveler. It's probably why I trust you."

Morning crests. It's a subtle change to the quality of the sky, but it's enough that the rest of the caravan is roused. The moon remains low, nearly invisible as it shifts away from full. It wears a blueish tint; its color shifts seemingly at random. In the light of day, or what they call day, the caravan moves again, a single line of animals and people, three full wagons, a scattering of carts, the elephant at the back and the caravanner walking ahead. She carries a staff when she walks the sands, uses it as a walking stick, but also to sometimes block the glare of the moon, and sometimes in more arcane ways. She consults it sometimes like a navigator might use a sextant or compass. Their course behind them is a very straight line, but not without deviations.

From ahead, on the edge of the horizon that appears to be their destination, a lone rider approaches. They carry a lantern, to show they're not trying to be stealthy, and they ride with haste. They're coming straight to the caravan. From his position in the middle of the crowd, Jack Harlow appears not to express any direct interest. He looks, instead, to his east, where the Atlantic would be had he been on the coast of the United States. Another world, that.

It's an immense long stretch of sand, so the rider is visible for a long time. A sharpshooter might have taken a shot at any time. Any number of desert creatures might have snatched him from the sands. It's a dangerous place. Numbers imply safety.

When the rider finally reaches the caravan, he stops before the caravanner and dismounts. He bows. He's swathed in so many layers of robes, it's nearly operatic. He whispers, refers to the caravanner as a vizier, but even Jack Harlow cannot hear most of what he says.

He's still looking to the east, toward where the three shadowy figures have been lingering. He sees no one now, just the dry, dusted expanse.

After a few minutes, the caravanner calls for the caravan to circle around her. "There's trouble ahead," she tells them. "A city has fallen."

"What does that mean, fallen?" someone asks.

"Governors, kings, emperors come and go," she says. "Babylon has changed hands."

This causes a wave of murmuring, which she allows. No one says anything to Jack Harlow. Even among outcasts, he's the outsider.

When it quiets, the caravanner says, "I shall go ahead, to ensure our safety. I'd like a single volunteer to come with me." She looks straight at Jack Harlow. Others whisper, or shy away, and one or two take a breath to offer their services.

He wants to say no. He wants to say nothing at all. Jack Harlow would prefer to melt into the background, into the crowd, into a place of invisibility, but such places never truly provided sanctuary. Slowly, the others back down, even those who might have been anxious to try their luck in Babylon. With a sigh that's not as heavy as it should it be, Jack Harlow walks to the center of the circle to face the caravanner. "I suppose you mean me."

"And no one else," she tells him.

"You've manufactured this," he says. "I'm not the power you think I am."

"Power?" she asks, with a smile that shows in her eyes. "It's not a question of power. It's a question of trust."

The rest of the caravan regroups to continue its trek. The rider will stay with them and guide them toward Babylon, the next stop on their itinerary. The caravanner leads two of the camels away, has them unloaded of all they carry, that weight redistributed amongst the other animals and carts.

"Don't we need provisions?"

"If you're hungry," she says, "eat before we ride."

"I'm good."

They mount the camels, who seem not to even notice their weight. "We'll make one stop on the way," the caravanner tells him. "From there, we'll be less than half a day from the gates of Babylon."

They ride.

2.

The ride is long, but not arduous. The camel isn't the most comfortable ride—it's certainly no Mustang—but it doesn't take long for Jack to get used to it. They ride under the pale moon like a Cheshire cat. They ride swiftly, so that the caravan disappears in the dust behind them.

The desert is mostly deserted, which has been their experience since Jack Harlow joined with the caravan. The sands stretch forever in all directions, though there are rock formations that must be the edge of mountains barely visible in the haze of the west.

There's no opportunity for conversation as they ride. The camels move too fast, too jerkily, to allow it. They blow through a wind of their own making, so only raised voices would be heard. And Jack Harlow doesn't want to give up his secrets to the desert.

They stop at a copse of cacti—primarily saguaro, the only kind Jack had ever been familiar with as a child, and that from cartoons. He'd spent most his life east of the Mississippi, often hugging the coastline even as he ran away from all the things he'd been able to see, so desert was not a familiar terrain to him.

From her robes, the caravanner withdraws a massive machete, a killing weapon, huge and sharp and glinting even in the gray light of this desert. She cuts away the fruit of one of the smaller cacti, then cuts it in half and gives one part to Jack.

"It won't taste good," she says, "but you'll dehydrate without some water."

"Is it safe?"

"Is anything?" She tears a piece of the fruit away and pops it into her mouth. She chews for a bit, then turns to spit out the fleshy part. "Oh, and don't swallow the fruit. Just the water."

He follows her lead. As he chews, the juices of the fruit roll down his throat. It's sweet, but also pungent and acrid. Eventually, he's sucked the liquid out of the fruit, leaving only the meaty part burning like acid on his tongue. He spits it out, then asks, "You live on this?"

She shakes her head. "Only when we must. There's no true oasis between us and Babylon, and this is where we'll make camp for the night."

The gray sky has darkened, but Jack is never sure of the time of day. "I can ride further."

"So can I," she says, "but we should conserve energy for tomorrow, because I do not know what will greet us at the gate."

"Who do you think I am?" Jack Harlow asks.

She looks at him. This time, if she smiles, it doesn't reach her eyes, and the scarf across the lower half of her face hides it. She says, "Who do you think I am?"

"They call you the caravanner."

"They call me a great many things, when they think I cannot hear them," she says. She reaches behind her head and unties the scarf, revealing the rest of her face, red lips and one jagged white scar on the side. "They say I'm a monster under my mask."

"Why do you wear it, then?" Jack asks.

"It's good, to let them foster their own beliefs," she says. "Help me tie the camels to the cacti, and we'll set up blankets for our beds."

Despite that she had said no provisions, a small pack had remained on the back of one of the camels. Jack hadn't noticed it. From inside, she withdraws rope and two thin blankets.

It's only a few minutes of work to set up their makeshift camp. Far behind them, the caravan has probably also settled for the night. To their right, the east, Jack sees shapes on the horizon.

"So," the caravanner says, "it's you they follow, not the prisoner. That's good to know."

"Is that why you separated us?" Jack asks.

"You keep wanting to ascribe ulterior motives. No, I separated us because I think I'd prefer you at my side at the gates of Babylon over anyone else."

"Why is that?"

"Because of your eyes. The way they watch, the way they seek. And because I know what you are, or what you were, in the long ago. You have travelled with us a long while, but you've never asked for my name."

"You've never asked mine."

"You wouldn't tell me the truth," she says. "I don't know what you're running from, or what you're searching for, but like the fairies of the old tales, you believe in the power of naming things."

He's been naming things in the dark since the night of his seventeenth birthday.

"So I'll give you mine," she says. "It's nothing special, and unlike yours, will mean nothing to anyone. It gives you no power over me, but it's not something I share freely with every random rogue who hitches a ride with my caravan. My name, my true name, which I've carried since birth, is Asteria."

"I don't believe your claim that names are meaningless."

"I was named for the quail island," she says, "because my mother, knowing my future, thought it would be ironic."

"What future did she know?"

When Asteria smiles, it's radiant. "Desert sands."

Jack nods. Above, the clouds have shifted their shapes and thickened.

"Yes," Asteria says, shaking her head, "a storm is coming. But we will not be finding shelter. It'll rain, as it does every rainy season, for half the night, not more."

"Jack Harlow," he tells her. "My name."

"Your name does carry meaning," she tells him. "You do well, keeping it close."

"I don't like to draw attention to myself."

"Ah, but attention is drawn, nonetheless," she says. "Sleep, Jack Harlow. I'll take the first watch. When the rain is too much for you, then you can take watch, and I'll sleep."

Jack Harlow doesn't sleep deeply. He doesn't remember ever being able to truly do so, not since he was a teenager, not since before he knew ghosts were real and not alone in the dark. But he does approach something like sleep, for what it's worth. He doesn't sleep deeply enough for dreams. It's been a long time. When he approaches that state, the heat of his dreams, the redness of them, jars him awake. That happens again tonight. He's just about to see something, to maybe learn something—he doesn't know what, and he doesn't want to know, though of course he desperately wants to—and suddenly it's raining ice needles on his face.

The rain is cold and relentless. Asteria stands near him, near the camels, scanning the horizon. "I can't see far," she says. "Not with the mist of the storm." Lightning arcs across the sky, followed almost immediately by a boom of thunder to rival every storm on earth. "To be honest," she says, "I'm surprised you slept as long as you did."

Jack Harlow stretches, yawns, opens his mouth to swallow the rain. It's cleaner than the cactus water, fresher, colder. It's the first rain he remembers since—that's hard to say—since the night he died, and the night the ghost of him died. He's lost track of time.

"I wasn't always alone," Jack says, more to himself than to the caravanner. She seems to know this, though, and offers no response. "Do you know what happened? How I ended up in the desert?"

"Misfortune and misadventure."

"More precisely."

She shakes her head. "I'm no seer, Jack Harlow."

"What are you?"

"More names, is that it?" she asks. "No, I'm just the caravanner. The marshal charged with transport of that prisoner."

"Who's the prisoner?"

She shakes her head again. "I can't tell you that. Now give me that blanket. I'll wake when the storm has passed, and we'll make dust to Babylon."

She takes the blanket, wraps it once around herself, and closes her eyes. He believes she's immediately asleep.

The storm rages. Lightning flies across the sky. Thunder rumbles. The rain doesn't stop, and there's no place to get away from it. The cacti offer no shelter. Indeed, in the flashes of lightning, he sees the silhouette of a body hanging from one of the highest arms of the cactus, a hanged man, the position reminding him of his father—but it's not his father. It's something of a road sign, a calling card, an indication of where they are— even if Jack Harlow doesn't understand the implications. Someone has died here, maybe many someones, possibly as acts of justice.

The horizons are much closer in the darkness of the storm. The clouds above are so thick, he can almost reach up into the storm. Lightning dances across many layers of cloud stuff, some of it close enough the electricity prickles the short hairs on his arms and the back of his neck.

To the west, the foothills leading to mountains are lost in the murk. To the east, whoever follows him hides without hiding. They could be close, half the distance as during the day. He watches for any signs of movement, but it's all movement; the wind, the clouds, even the desert kicked up by the falling rain. There's almost no point in keeping watch. If someone sneaks up on them, it'll be a surprise to them both.

The storm twists shadows, giving shape to shapelessness, form to formlessness, obscuring anything and everything that comes close. Jack Harlow, even diminished, even far from his full strength, sees better than most, but his eyes cannot penetrate the walls of darkness surrounding them. He watches ground and sky, he feels for tremors in the ground, he realizes he'll never see what's coming.

But something comes.

For a while, he watches the caravanner, Asteria, sleeping on her side, her body barely moving with her shallow breathing, seemingly unperturbed by the ceaseless freezing rain. For Jack, it's like torture, something that will never end, a constant reminder of the night he'd failed.

He sees echoes of the DarkCrawler, but only scaped against the back of his mind. He sees Lisa Sparrow's body repurposed to the DarkCrawler's twisted vision, but her soul—her ghost—her spirit—the essential part of her—was already gone. He sees Nick Hunter and the Lady Chandra, Jia Li, Kalinda, his sister, his mother.

When Asteria opens her eyes, she's fully and completely awake in an instant, responding to the slightest relent of the storm. He asks, "Is the prisoner my mother?"

"No."

She gathers the blanket as Jack unties the camels. The storm is letting up, but far from over. There's no point in resting if neither of them has any rest left in them. The camels object rudely, but quickly concede, and they're bound again for Babylon.

Jack Harlow knows nothing of the Babylon here, though a place on Long Island shared the name. The

Tower of Babel was supposed to be there, wasn't it? And the hanging gardens. His knowledge is slim and inconsequential. Whatever he thinks he knows, it won't matter.

They don't race across the desert during the storm. The camels' footing remains sure, but Asteria tells him there's a chance of flash flooding, there's a chance the river will overflow. He doesn't know what river she means. There's a possibility the sand will become weak and suck them into the center of the earth.

Their camels stop because they have no choice.

A flash of lightning reveals they are surrounded by warriors on horses and camels and other creatures Jack doesn't recognize. They carry banners, swords, spears, shields.

Jack and Asteria are, with the exception of one machete, at least as far as Jack knows, unarmed.

"Trespassers," one of the warriors says. They're big, ugly men, scarred mutants, their faces a mess of asymmetry, their bodies hunched, their muscles bulging unnaturally. They're only visible in the flashes of lightning. They shift and move around them, so Jack Harlow cannot get an accurate count. One dozen? Two?

When he thought he was a watcher, they would've left him alone. He was untouchable. But he'd never been right about that. When he thought he was the DarkWalker, all-powerful and ever getting stronger, he could've dispatched them with little more effort than a thought. Sent some to other realms, cut some down at the knees, dissolved the glue that held their cells together, reversed their skin and their organs— sometimes without even meaning to do it.

He isn't sure if he is prepared to fight. He rides across the desert with the caravanner and her tribe because what else is there to do?

"Merely travelers," Asteria says. "Here and gone."

"Vagabonds," one of the others says.

"Thieves." It's spit out like a curse, like it's the final decision.

For a moment, there's only the sound of thunder. The glint of metal in the lightning. The sudden stopping of the rain.

One of the horses carries its warrior one step closer. "Any last requests?"

The caravanner merely spits back a word: "*Marauders*."

The marauder who had asked came forward. Asteria cuts him down, severing his head with a single stroke of the machete. The horse rears and runs off. Her camel never even seemed to move.

"Next?" she asks.

They don't hesitate. They come in as one.

Asteria moves like a dervish, like she's made of desert sand and wind, like she's a force of nature. She spins off her camel, slashes the throat of one marauder then another, ducks under their spears and swords, hops over the horse of another and removes his arm just below the shoulder.

One of the warriors attempts to go for Jack. For just a moment, he stops watching the caravanner. He catches the blade in his hand. It hurts. It cuts him, though it doesn't cut through him. He twists the blade around, yanks the warrior off his horse. He's still amazed at the strength he retains. He plunges the weapon back, penetrating the warrior's chest with the blunt end of the weapon, before releasing it.

Asteria circles around to them. He's the only of the marauders not dead. She's gone through them all. Blood still pours from the machete. She stands over the warrior with the dull end of a spear protruding from his chest, holds the machete to the barely visible flesh of his neck, and asks, "Any last requests?"

She doesn't give him time to answer.

Jack Harlow stares as she wipes blood off her blade on the cloth of the marauder. She looks back, grins through her scarf—he recognizes the expression through her eyes—and says, "After the things I've heard about you, Jack Harlow, I'm surprised you look so shocked."

"That was brutal," Jack says. "Why ask if he has requests?"

"Marauders only ever ask to die," she says. "It's against their religion, to be defeated in combat." She hides the machete in a sheath somewhere under her robes. "You might call it something of a mercy, that I didn't make him beg for death." She mounts her camel, winks at Jack Harlow, and says, "Babylon awaits."

3.

They ride only a few hours before the city starts to become visible. It's surrounded by a wall, so that's what they see: a massive wall that blends well with the desert. As they get closer, the quality of the sand and sky change, and the grays shift toward light brown. It's subtle, and incomplete, but noticeable. Babylon intrudes upon the desert.

It's a massive city, and a massive wall, easily five or six stories tall. Like Asteria, the colors of the wall blend with the desert, and it's almost impossible to know when he actually began to see the city.

"It's hidden?" Jack asks.

"Yet you can see it."

"As you said, I have eyes."

"And I," Asteria says, "was born here."

But this isn't an earthly realm, not exactly, and this was never a Babylon you could find there. Even once they see the walls, it's a while before they reach them. The massive gates, however, are closed.

"Babylon born," Asteria tells the gate keeper, who stares out from the smallest possible window twenty feet up the wall. She bares her wrist and shows its tattoo. Jack gets only a quick glimpse; it's basically a silhouette of these gates opened. It might or might not be a good thing to announce; Jack has no idea what kind of ruler has taken over, and how well they might or might not tolerate the city's citizens.

But it seems enough for the gate keeper. He signals to someone, who presumably signals to someone else, and eventually a small door in the gate—not the entirety of the gate itself—is pushed open from within. The door is big enough for the camels, but only after they dismount. The animals are taken by a gateman.

"They'll be fine," Asteria tells Jack.

"That tattoo," Jack says. "It's not given to everyone born in Babylon, is it?"

"No." She keeps her mask on in the city. The avenues are crowded with traders jostling to sell their wares, performing tricksters, pickpockets, and musicians. "You would fit right in," she tells him.

But he wouldn't. He doesn't like the glory they seek; however, he comes to realize they're all selling something, they're all surviving by scraping, and only those who aren't seeking attention actually draw it. Like the man with the super dark skin and glowing eyes who stands aside, away from the activity, yet Jack can't help but notice him.

Of course, Asteria also walks straight toward him.

Within arm's length of each other, she stops, they both cross their arms—showing wrist tattoos, his being a phoenix—and give the slightest bow of the head. Then he smiles, and she throws an arm around him. Jack hears when she whispers, "How is mother?"

"Content, as always," he says, before they let go. He then looks at Jack Harlow, looks him up and down like appraising a side of meat. "My birds whisper about a man like you," he tells Jack. "Come, let's get inside before we attract too much attention."

Inside happens to be a large building with an enclosed courtyard. They go through a kitchen area to get to the courtyard, where they are surrounded by marble statues painted in vibrant blues and reds and golds. The courtyard is large enough to get lost in, though the labyrinth of paths seems straightforward enough, and the greenery—which is lush, considering they are still in the desert—seems low and meticulously kept.

The man leads them to a square of benches. "Sit," he says, taking a seat while holding Asteria's hands and forcing her to sit with him. He's more than he appears to be. "First, tell me: is the prisoner safe?"

"Of course."

"And the silks? The spices?"

"Abundant," she says. "It was a good harvest."

"And the caravan?"

"Scoundrels, rascals, killers, scum," she says, "and this one." She nods toward Jack. He's trying to keep his attention on anything else—the statues of goddesses, the shimmering sun, the scent of jasmine—but it's a lie and they all know it.

"This one," the man says.

Jack says, primarily to Asteria, "This doesn't seem like you described."

She's smiling as she removes the scarf from her face. "It's not. It was all a lie. A ruse. To separate you from the company of—well, essentially, thieves."

"What for?"

She shakes a head. "Their destiny and yours do not connect," she says. "Mother will explain."

"Mother's been waiting to see you," the man says. "Another DarkWalker, in the flesh, so to say."

"Another?"

"You're not the first," he tells Jack.

Jack looks to Asteria. "You knew who I was already."

"I did."

So much for all that talk about trust. Jack Harlow sighs. He is tired—tired of running, tired of fighting, tired of being lied to and cheated, tired of people and things trying—in some cases successfully—to kill him. "Sure, whatever," he says. "Take me to her."

The man shakes his head. "No need for taking you anywhere. She'll come when she's ready."

Jack Harlow leans over. "Do you know how many people and things I've killed without meaning to?" It's low, and meant to be something of a threat.

The man shakes his head. "Tell me, though. I love a good story."

"Babylon," Asteria adds, "is known for its stories."

Jack leans back.

"There's a story of a jinn-taught girl who escaped Babylon in the days before the war, though time was and is always funny here. It was a great and terrible war, a recent war, that she escaped, and she brought death with her wherever she went. But before she escaped, there was a child who was a hunter, and wanted his father's bow."

"Shush," Asteria says. "Everyone knows that story."

"He is a stranger," the man says.

"The story doesn't end happily," Asteria says. "The boy kills his father with a magic bow, and the jinn-taught girl teaches him a lesson about how untrustworthy she is. All children in Babylon know the story."

"Are you telling me I made a mistake in trusting you?" Jack Harlow asks.

She shakes her head. "You don't trust me. You're just waiting for what's next. I didn't need to, and I didn't want to mislead you. But here you are, because that's what Mother required of me."

Jack Harlow leans back. Takes a breath. Glances at the grayish moon, the sepia tone of the sky. If he doesn't look directly at her, he doesn't even see Asteria; she blends with her surroundings even more perfectly within the walls of Babylon.

"I thought," the man says, "you were going to tell us a story."

"I don't even know who you are."

"Oh." The man seems taken aback. "I am Al-Qaum. I'm sorry, I thought you knew that, you being Jack Harlow of the Tiger."

Jack shakes his head. "Not *of the Tiger*," he says. It's the organization his father had belonged to, or maybe ran.

"I told you, brother," Asteria says, swatting his leg.

"A story, then," Al-Qaum says, "of who you really are. We have—well, we have however long we have, surely long enough for a tale."

When Jack doesn't immediately launch into telling a story, Asteria says, "All of his stories have bad endings. He's the DarkWalker. It's part of his nature."

"No, no," Al-Qaum says. "That cannot be true." He leans toward Jack, putting his hands on his knees to support his weight. "I know there's a love story at the heart of it all, isn't there? A woman? A sparrow? We only get bits of the tale here, and I'd truly love to hear the whole thing."

Jack looks at him. It must be quite a look, because the man leans back and holds up both palms and says, "Of course, you can tell whatever story you wish. I won't mind."

"Stories," Asteria says to Jack, "are all we have, and all we are, in the desert and in Babylon, and in any other place, as well. So we trade them."

"Trade, then," Jack says. "You tell me something first."

"Don't be rude."

"It's okay," Al-Qaum says. "As you say, he's a stranger to our land. I will tell you a story, a quick little tale, if that's what you want. And then, I hope, you'll tell yours."

4.

In a golden age, when the sky was bright and full of color and depth, the gods of old waged war over things like beauty, and never before had there been a beauty such as Anastasia. She was rare, and radiant, and lovely in every way, and she was kind to everyone. She wasn't a princess or a priestess, just the daughter of a baker, and she aspired to be nothing more than a baker like her father.

But she caught the eye of sun gods, moon gods, hunter gods, all of them, and they began delivering gifts. Simple things at first: a basket of fruits that never ran out or went rotten; a dress of silk that changed its shape and color at the whim of its wearer; a spider seamstress, barrels of wine, chests full of gold, and finally, one day, an opal in the shape of a heart, a fire opal, all black with red and green veined through it.

This was a special jewel, had been a gift onto one of the fairest of the goddesses, and how it had been stolen from her treasure rooms is an unknown story. But stolen, it was, and some of the gods considered this an affront to their very nature. As I said, wars had been fought over beauty. And this time, at the center of it, was a mortal, Anastasia, who had done nothing but walk in the rain, bathe in the sunlight, dance under the moon.

The gods are often petty, and their rivalries run deep, so when sides are taken, there's no telling how or why, but the wars they wage are often legendary. Anastasia fled, trying to escape the worst of it. You must remember, human armies were often tools of the gods, and tens of thousands died when the gods went to war. She wanted no part of this. She spurned all suitors, godly or otherwise. She went north, first, to the lands of snow and ice, to sleep under the aurora, but eventually even the ice giants took note of her beauty. With help, she fled to other realms.

Some of the other realms are older than history.

Anastasia arrived in Babylon, a young city then, if it can ever be said to be young, and took to wearing the mask to hide her beauty from the gods and the people.

Despite this, they called her the mother of monsters. They locked her away in dungeons for centuries. She ranted and raged, she fought, she killed, and she escaped whenever she wished. She had been deemed too beautiful by the gods to ever die. She considered this a curse. She descended to the lowest levels of Babylon, to the lowest levels of hell realms, seeking anything that might break her curse and allow her to die.

She learned, eventually, that death was not an end, merely a transition from one place to another, and that she could already travel across those veils and boundaries. So she returned to her prison under Babylon, and even now walks its streets in the sketchy twilight that has overrun the city.

That twilight is a story for another time, but I have left one thing out of Anastasia's tale, one important thing. Her journeys were numerous, her adventures fill volumes of stories for children and adults. But on one of these journeys, she met a creature that might, indeed, be capable of ending her life, an entity more powerful than the gods. She wrestled with this creature, she cajoled it, she tormented it, she loved it, and she hated it. Anastasia begged and pleaded, but the creature—you know what kind of creature I mean—refused. It would decimate nations, destroy entire civilizations, and laugh at her because she was spared every time.

The crime, of course, was a genocide, the destruction of Atlantis. It took the combined effort of a hundred thousand sorcerers, gods and godlings, alchemists, silversmiths, medicine people, and storytellers just to build a prison that would hold that creature. Ever since, she has sought another of its kind, another like it, another that might be capable of killing beauty.

JOHN URBANCIK

5.

Al-Qaum finishes his story and leans back.

"That story was for you," Asteria says, "because you're the next chapter."

"You think I'll be able to kill someone who cannot be killed?"

"We know you have done so in the past," Asteria says.

"There are stories of you on Mount Armageddon," Al-Qaum adds.

"In Shangri La."

"In the Silver Blade."

"Under the earth."

"Over the moon."

"Those stories," Jack Harlow says, "aren't completely true. And some of those places—I've never been over the moon."

"Time is strange in Babylon," Asteria says. "Ruined by ancient ways, you might say. But now you owe us a story in return."

Jack Harlow sighs. "Fine," he says. "Once upon a time, there was a man—no, I was a boy then—who wanted only to be left alone. Nobody listened to him. A lot of people died because of it. The end."

Al-Qaum laughs. Asteria frowns. She says, "That's not much of a story."

"But it's a true one," Jack says.

"You promised a love story," Al-Qaum says.

"I promised nothing."

"It was implicit."

Asteria adds, "You know the importance of balance. Don't risk imbalance today, Jack Harlow."

He closes his eyes. He doesn't know what else to do. He adds to his story: "One day, the boy—no, he was a man by then, but not a god, though he would later mistake himself for one—he met a woman whose beauty was incomparable, whose spirit was indomitable, whose essence was all things pure to all the things inside him that were ruined. When they met, they filled the holes in each other, they healed each other's hurts, they—sang songs worthy of legend, but only to each other. They faced armies in the dark, legions of creatures with death at the front of their minds, and in the end she—because of her inherent goodness—sacrificed herself to protect his life and soul."

"She was the sparrow?" Al-Qaum asks.

"No," Jack says. "That was her name. Lisa Sparrow."

"It sounds true," Al-Qaum says, "but you have much to learn about storytelling."

Jack Harlow doesn't respond to this. "Your Mother," he says, "is Anastasia, and she believes..."

"What she believes," Al-Qaum says, "is her business. Ask her when she arrives."

"Is she your mother?" Jack asks.

"She's everyone's mother, in Babylon," he says. "She's the source of all that is good and beautiful in this city, and the source of all that is dark and shadowy, all that is sharp, all that is smooth. She is, in essence, the mother of the city, because it is said the city was built specifically to be her home, even if it was built before she'd been born."

At this point, the storm has ended. The last of the lightning has finished its dance, the thunders have rolled far into the distance, the rain is done, and the rain-wet ground is already dry in places. Things move quickly in the desert; or, as Al-Qaum suggested, time flows weirdly.

"You didn't have to kidnap me," Jack says. "I would've come willingly."

"You might've," Al-Qaum says. "You might not have."

"And I didn't kidnap you," Asteria points out. "We fought the marauders side by side, we made haste together through the desert, we shared the fruit of the desert, and we passed a night together under the storm. There was no point where I, or anyone, forced you to do anything, Jack Harlow. Do not forget that. You *did* come willingly."

He can't argue against that. "You lied to me."

"Everybody lies," she says. "You know this. Even you, coming into the desert unarmed—so you claim—that is a lie."

"You are a power," Al-Qaum says. "If you wished, you could dissolve us, this house, this entire city, with nothing but a thought."

"I knew the risk," Asteria says, "before we found you in the desert."

"You found me on purpose?"

She nods.

Above them, the sky brightens.

Anastasia, the mother, arrives.

6.

When Anastasia enters the courtyard, all the grays in the sky and the bricks melt away, revealing brighter, more vibrant colors. She wears a full head scarf that hides everything but eyes like faceted suns, glistening and glimmering, perhaps the center of her beauty. Her dress is a thousand layers of veils, each thin and nearly transparent, the overall affect being overwhelming. It hints at the shape of her while covering all of her; it reveals nothing except promise and hope and magnificence.

Jack Harlow rises when Al-Qaum and Asteria stand, but he doesn't bow like they do. Their deference has been learned or earned, but he's unable to do anything. It's an effort, briefly, just to maintain his own identity.

When she walks, the winds glide around her. When she smiles, even under the scarves—not a single headscarf, but numerous thin layers applied with structure and deliberation, each layer like gossamer in another sensuous hue of gold and indigo and jade and crimson—when she smiles, he can see—maybe in her eyes, maybe because her expressions are a power of their own and no garment, no matter how extravagant, can hide them.

She walks like a god. Even the gods cannot kill her. Presumably, some have tried.

She sits on the stone bench next to Jack Harlow. She pats the seat so that he might remember where to sit again himself. The others, they accept the briefest of acknowledgements and return to their bench. Jack, having taken a moment to regain himself, sits. He's afraid to look straight into her eyes, but she takes his hands, one in each of hers, and says, "You will help me."

It's not a question. Her voice is an imperative. It's smooth like honey, deep like bourbon, and he can imagine the shape of her lips as she forms the words. She speaks with deliberation, as though they have all the time in the world and more. Her hands are smooth, her fingernails dazzlingly kaleidoscopic, a perfect match for her eyes, which he finally finds himself looking into.

There's a long moment. He feels himself tumbling, as if into a black hole, but it's filled with warmth and love and hope and promise, and something inside him breaks. Something inside him hitches, gets caught and entangled, even ruined. A part of him dies, looking into her eyes, a part of him that was sick, deeply buried, slimy, even gross, an oily patch on his soul holding back his regrets, his fears, his anger.

It's a thin layer, actually, between that and the reality around him.

Jack Harlow cries.

Holding Anastasia's hands, trapped within her eyes, his tears fall without control. He can do nothing to hold them back, so he lets them fall silently. They're warm and wet on his cheeks, and when they drop to the sand, the desert absorbs them.

For a while, Anastasia only smiles. Then she leans closer, and presses her lips onto the corner of his right eye, taking a tear from its source. She kisses his left eye next, then leans back, leaving cold spots where her mouth had touched him, and says again, softer this time, "You will help me." This time, it's almost a question, but it's actually a confirmation. As though Jack had agreed to hand over his very soul.

"I am glad you love another," she says, looking down at their hands. "You're rare, so beautiful a creature of darkness."

He closes his eyes. Not to break the spell, as nothing will ever do that. He closes his eyes to stem the tide of emotion, the wave of sorrow washing over and through him, the agony of all he's lost.

She kisses his lips. It's not sexual. It's something else, something transcendental, something thoroughly wonderful. She stirs no feelings of want or longing or desire; she only ignites memories, wishes fulfilled, and hope—something he thought he'd lost.

7.

Jack Harlow wakes in a soft bed surrounded by pillows and blankets. There's the sound of water, the scents of jasmine and vanilla, and utter darkness.

"It can be night, inside," Anastasia says, supporting his back as he rises to sit, giving him a chalice filled with—water, by the taste of it. "Where I'm sure you're more comfortable."

"Where are we?" he asks.

"We haven't left Babylon."

"Who are you?" Jack blinks, though there's nothing to be seen in the total darkness except an iridescent hint of her eyes. It's not the right question. "What are you?"

"My name is Anastasia," she says, "and you've already heard my story. One of my stories. There are, in fact, so many, and none are completely accurate." During a pause, Jack swallows more of the water. It's the smoothest, iciest, most hedonistic water he's ever tasted. "As to what I am—it's simplest to say I am a creature of the light. Just as you are of the night."

"You're beautiful," Jack says.

"It's good, to get that out of your system."

"I don't understand what happened."

"You're so accustomed to fighting, to conflict, to death and destruction. When faced with something outside your experience, albeit not completely, your body shut itself down."

"I passed out?"

"In essence."

"I didn't even realize it."

"You're safe here, in this house, in this city," she says. "This is, admittedly, a transitionary place, neither purely of night or day. You might call it a twilight place. But you're safe, because the two strongest powers known in the other realms, the power of the DarkWalker and the power of Beauty epitomized, are in league. No one, no one at all, would dare challenge us."

"Why do you need my help?" Jack asks. "It's not because you want to die."

"No," she says, "though that's a part of it, in a way. But it's better, now, if you rest, if you prepare for the journey ahead of us. Because while I say we are two of the most powerful forces to ever exist, that's not entirely factual. You are twice diminished, Jack Harlow, DarkWalker, Destroyer of Hells. And I—I am fading."

Jack tries to swing his legs off the bed, but she holds him in place with a single hand on his back. "You have nothing to worry about, or to fear, in this place, Jack Harlow," she whispers, her lips—bare, not hidden beneath a thousand ethereal layers, are near enough to his ear that it makes him dizzy. "You're safe with me."

He realizes then that she's completely nude, not hidden from him at all except for the lack of light. Her eyes are the only light, but they're not enough to see by. They only reveal her face. And her expression. It's an expression of love, of warmth and kindness, of things Jack Harlow finds difficult to understand. She kisses him, gently pressing him back down to the bed, and he's unwilling to resist. She's not like any other woman he's ever been with. She's a goddess of beauty in the flesh, and she's skilled in a thousand and one methods of love, many of which he'd never imagined. It's soft, it's gentle, and it's long-lasting. Her flesh under his hands, over his body, against his mouth—is a dream in the darkness. He lets go of regrets, loses touch with the fears inside him, and for a moment, in the darkness hidden away from the twilight of Babylon, he feels there's two of him, two separate entities, one of darkness and one of joy. He didn't know such a thing could even exist, certainly not inside of him. When they orgasm, it's like a galaxy shatters inside him, unleashing all its power and heat into his soul, the light of thousands of stars, thousands of suns, and he can no longer distinguish between the light and the darkness.

CHAPTER TWO

1.

Time has no meaning in Babylon. When Jack Harlow wakes again, it might be years later. He doesn't know and doesn't care. He's still got that feeling of being outside of himself. It's disconcerting, sitting alone in the darkness, knowing he's sitting with himself and, this time, no one else. He hears nothing, not even the sound of his other's breath, because there is no one physically in the room with him.

In the dark, able to see nothing, not even his own hand in front of his face, he says, "So, Jack Harlow, this is where your path has led you. Babylon. An other realm that maybe doesn't exist back home. What would your mother say?"

What would she say indeed? The last time he saw her, she wasn't herself. She'd been under the influence of the DarkCrawler, and she'd said things no mother should ever say to a child, even the least favorite of your children. Amelia Harlow whispering in the storm of Shangri La—words not even her daughter next to her could hear—but then that final plea: *Believe nothing he says*.

Even, he has to assume, when the DarkCrawler uses his mother's mouth to say the words.

"And what about Lisa?" he asks the darkness. There's no one to answer except himself. "Have you forgotten her? Lost her forever? Where has she gone? If the DarkCrawler displayed her body so horrifically in Shangri La just for your benefit, her spirit must have somehow escaped him. Where has she gone?"

Silence fills the darkness.

Silence, and the ghost of himself, his own echoes, the pieces he has never been able to track. "You're the DarkWalker," he tells himself in the dark. "You went through hells looking for her, but you went to all the wrong places. She never left the apartment. She convinced you to leave. She knew you would stay and waste away."

It's good, to have this frank conversation with himself. He might not have been able to do this yesterday. "Find her. Hone in on her. She's out there somewhere, maybe lost, maybe just unable to go after you. But she still loves you, and you love her. She crossed countless other realms in her journey to Shangri La, following a thread—a thread she could see, that you could, briefly, see as well. You're diminished, but you're still the DarkWalker, and that makes you..."

He stops there. It's a tough word to say, the next one, so he hesitates over it; he inhales and exhales several times; he rolls the word across the edges of his tongue. Finally, he decides it's the right word, and maybe it's a gift from Anastasia that he can say it: "*Extraordinary.*"

And it's true. He's something rare, something unique—it's time to accept that.

He'd rather not be, but it's too late for that.

He closes his eyes and concentrates. He had followed the threads that connected Lisa Sparrow to her apartment, where she had died and where she had returned to life. That hadn't ever been entirely true. But there had also been a thread connecting her to him. He'd been too blind to see it then, too full of himself, too unsure of his abilities.

There are, indeed, numerous threads connected to him, people throughout the world, beyond the world, through all the realms, infernal places and paradises alike. He touches a thread. It hums gently, maybe only a sound he hears inside his head. It's the most recent thread, two of them intertwined, in fact, leading back to Anastasia. Another pair of threads go back to Asteria and to Al-Qaum.

Others go to Naomi, now in Haiti; to Jia Li, currently deep in the jungles of Tibet; to Kalinda, ever in Shangri La. Others are not so easily trackable. Nick Hunter. His father and sister, both dead, both gone. His mother. The thread connecting him to Lisa Sparrow, however, is weak, almost non-existent.

He gets up. Gathers his clothes and dresses. He's comfortable in the dark, even when he cannot see. When he opens the door to leave, an enormous amount of sunlight spills into the room from the hall. There are skylights everywhere, and tunnels that seem to bend the light around corners. Only the one room is awash in darkness. Maybe they had built the room especially for him.

He finds the courtyard easily. In the center of the garden, surrounded by statues, walking paths, meditative stations, and stone benches, Anastasia is wrapped again in all her layers, dresses and scarves, everything to keep herself hidden. She looks up immediately when he steps into the courtyard. He feels the potency of her smile.

"Jack Harlow," she says, beckoning with a finger. "Come, walk with me."

The garden, the entire courtyard, seems larger today—whether compared to yesterday or weeks ago, Jack cannot be certain. The path is broad enough for him and Anastasia to walk side by side.

"You have questions," she says. "Please, don't take offence, but I heard you talking with yourself."

He wants to defend it, to say something, but she doesn't give him the chance. "I often discuss important matters with myself, though I usually take care that not even the wind can carry my words. You were loud, Jack Harlow. I'm surprised—but also, I understand."

"You're not what I expected."

"It's rare that anyone is who you expect them to be." She smiles again, touches his arm, and shows him one of the brighter, bluer flowers. "Do you know what this is?"

"I don't."

She shakes her head. "It's a flower, Jack Harlow. Doesn't it smell delicious?"

"Like—a perfume, I think."

"We're in the cradle of civilization here," she tells him. "This is where life began, or is said to have begun, though it's not entirely accurate. But you know the strength of stories, I'm sure."

"I do."

"I will tell you a story one day," she says, "but I fear your time in Babylon is at an end."

"Why would you say that?"

"You don't hide it well, Jack Harlow. You itch to get moving again. You're unafraid of who might be pursuing you."

"Does someone pursue me?"

She ignores the question. "But you are in pursuit, yourself. You want to finish your love story."

"I wouldn't use those words."

"No, of course not," she says. "Here, this is Aphrodite, the Greek goddess of love. It's not actually her, trapped within the stone, but there's someone, an entity, something occupying this marble flesh. Can you feel it?"

He touches the statue—her arm, for modesty's sake. Underneath, there's a faint trace of blood flow, a rhythm of breath. "I can."

"You became so strong so quickly," Anastasia tells him, "you never had a chance to develop. Now, as to your love story: you know all the greatest stories begin with *Once upon a time*, and that all the greatest stories end with *Happily ever after*."

"I don't know if that's true," Jack admits.

"It's not. It is another story we cling to. But that's

what I mean when I say you want to finish your love story. Not that you want it to end, but that you want to reach the point where the author says, *happily ever after*."

"I have to find Lisa," Jack says. "I don't know if she's in danger. I don't even know where she is. The thread that connects us—is weaker than I would expect."

"You're puzzled."

"Wouldn't you be?"

"As I said, you've never developed those kinds of senses. You think it means something, that only the strongest, most recent threads are visible to you. Let me tell you something, Jack Harlow. You're wrong. It means nothing, except that you're weak, weak in ways you've never been able to comprehend. But you won't always be weak, no matter what you think has happened. You are still a DarkWalker.

"And further," she says, stopping their walk and taking both his hands in hers, "I will help you. *We* will help you. Together, we will set out from Babylon and journey to whatever other realms we must to find your lost love."

JOHN URBANCIK

2.

The caravan reaches Babylon. The gates open wide to allow the wagons in. In the market, they trade some of the silks, some of the spices, for supplies they might need in the future. The prisoner's wagon is brought to the house and prepared, though Jack Harlow doesn't know what, exactly, is done.

The rest of the caravan, the criminals and creatures that had been wandering the desert with the caravanner—she remains unnamed for them, her face unseen—are given a choice. "You can come with us," she tells them, around a bonfire outside the gates, "or you can go about your business here. If and when I return, you'll be welcome to join with me again, but this promises to be a long and arduous journey, and there's a good chance you won't all survive."

That means different things to different people. Some wander off into the desert. Some disappear into the city. A few, however, stay.

"There's no promise of riches, either," she tells them. "There's no promise of reward, nor even thanks. We will be journeying through the other realms without hope of success, without hope of victory, without hope whatsoever."

One of the caravan says, "You say that like it's a bad thing."

In the evening, in the light of twilight—it's all twilight, even if not so gray in Babylon—they set out. There's a new wagon, locked, which no one has access to. Whispers spread quickly, though, that the mother of Babylon herself resides inside it. The prisoner's wagon remains calm and quiet throughout the first night of travel.

They travel by night. They travel by day. The desert out of Babylon is no longer the straight line it has been.

They head to the hills, toward the mountains, following a path the caravanner—Asteria—seems to know instinctually.

As they climb the mountain path, the air gets colder and thinner. Color returns to the world, but the colors are dark and muted: red rocks, deep blue skies, and true night when the time comes.

They travel for two full days and nights, until Babylon and the desert have disappeared entirely behind them, before breaking to set up camp.

In Babylon, they picked up a few new members of their troupe, Al-Qaum among them. They gather around a fire, which they do frequently when they stop, and stories are shared of the mountain pass and the other realms beyond.

"Giants live here," one person says. "Deep in slumber, they will nevertheless awaken one day, and they will want to return to their palaces in the clouds."

Another says, "The mountains are hollow, and the cities inside exist merely to keep the engines of the world running."

"The earliest gods came here first. They cast bones to divvy up the realms, and each was made from the imagination of one of those gods."

The caravanner and Jack Harlow walk around the perimeter of their little camp. It's uneven ground, hardly a clearing. They've got just two wagons now—the prisoner and the mother—and horses, though mostly they travel on foot. There's nothing to be seen from their vantage point except other parts of the mountains, rocks, crags, trees. Just two days, and they've left the desert behind them. The caravanner's robes have shifted their colors to keep her well camouflaged in the new environment. "Tell me," she says. "What do your eyes see?"

"Only mountains."

"Only?"

"Trees, clouds, us," he says. "I see drifting shadows, but they're paying us no mind. And I see hawks, chipmunks, that sort of thing."

"And your threads?"

Jack shrugs. There's not much to follow there, so he doesn't bother to say so.

"They tell stories of these mountains," she tells him, "but they're all just that—stories, weak, poorly told. Would you care to know whose mountains these are?"

"They belong to someone?"

"A tribe of seers."

"I've seen seers," Jack says. It's almost dismissive, not because he doubts their power—Kalinda is a seer, after all, and she keeps Shangri La; so, too, was Tania, in the Shallow City, where she'd kept control over the city through some sort of agreement with Jack Harlow's father—but because he's seen through their power.

"The tribe," the caravanner continues, "patrols their paths, and they won't let us pass if they don't want to allow it."

"Yet you led us straight here," Jack says.

"They've let me pass before. My major concern is you."

"The *DarkWalker*."

"These are twilight lands," she tells him.

"If they can see," Jack Harlow says, "then they know where I'm going and why, and maybe they know better than I do."

She points deep into the valley ahead of them. "You see that, there?"

At first, he doesn't see anything unusual; it's a broad valley. The path they're on seems to wind around the edges of it, never dipping too low—though many parts remain hidden, especially in the dark of night. "I see a hawk."

"Yes. Hawks. You've mentioned them already," the caravanner says. "They're the eyes of the seers."

"So they know we're coming?"

"They know we're here," the caravanner says. "It would be foolish, foolhardy, even risky, to assume they aren't also here."

"Which means?"

"Sleep with your eyes open, Jack Harlow."

Their patrol of the perimeter reveals nothing. Three of the troupe have returned successfully from a hunt, so there's meat to roast over the open flame. They tell their stories, they drink their wine—part of the provisions— and they sing their songs. Jack Harlow, sitting at the edge of all this, watches the valley, the hawks specifically, but sees nothing that disturbs or worries him.

Al-Qaum sits with him at one point and says, "Would you like a story to take you to the dreamlands?"

Jack Harlow smiles. It sounds so easy, like a sleeping pill, like a bottle of bourbon, like the mesmerizing eyes of somnambulists in the night. He takes a breath, nods, permitting Al-Qaum to tell him a story.

"Once, there was a king, whose lands stretched as far as he could see. He was just, and kind, and everyone loved him, but as he grew older, his vision failed him, until one morning he awoke and realized he was blind.

"He realized, then, through no fault of his own— though maybe it was diet, or maybe he had accidentally eaten a berry or a kind of mushroom he should have avoided—he had lost his kingdom. He set out on a journey to find himself, and his eyesight, and restore his realm. His guides took him to healers, but they were each and every one of them charlatans who took more of his money until he had nothing left. He visited the village elders, but in villages of criminals and vagabonds. His guides had been corrupted, or evil to begin with, and circled him through impossible lands without any hope of salvation. They wouldn't kill him outright, no, but finally, after many months of this, the blind king woke to find himself alone in the mountains.

"He fended for himself. He drank from the river. He ate berries. He became familiar with the land, with the brambles, with the caverns and holes in the rocky earth, until he could walk as sure-footedly as a mountain goat, even in his blindness. Some mornings, he found presents had been left for him in the night, mechanical birds, little piles of jewels, bouquets of flowers so fragrant they might cause a soul to fall instantly in love.

"One morning, he woke to find he wasn't alone. He was an old man, and she was young—but she was not human. She was a fairy, a kind of fairy, and she had tried a hundred times to lure him from his camp with lights in the forest. But he never saw the lights, and she never knew why.

"So she came close and asked, 'Why do you not follow the lights?'

"He smiled for her, though it may have been a sad smile, and showed her the clouds in his eyes. 'I see no lights,' he told her.

"She kissed him, a fairy's kiss in the light of the morning sun, once on each eye. He slept most of the day as his eyes healed, and when he woke, this old king, she was the first thing he saw.

"She asked him, 'Now, will you follow me into the mountain woods?' And he did. He followed her lights, her trail, her promises, and disappeared into the mountain woods, because she was the first thing he saw when he opened his eyes again and he'd fallen terribly in love."

"Terribly?" Jack Harlow asks.

Al-Qaum smiles. "Not all love is wondrous. Indeed,

not all love is love."

After a few moments of silence, Jack asks, "Is that the end of the king's story?"

Al-Qaum smiles and gets up to return to the bonfire. "I'm sure it's not."

As the night progresses and the bonfire dies down, most of the troupe sleeps. Always, two take guard, circling the perimeter, stationing themselves at higher vantage points. Jack Harlow sleeps, deeply and truly, but only for a short while. When he opens his eyes, he sees the fairy. She's bent over sharply and tilting her head to get a better look at him.

"Oh," she says, hopping back half a step. "You sleep ever so lightly."

"Who are you?" Jack asks.

"Shush, shush," she says, "or you'll alert the guards."

"Shouldn't I?"

"I mean you no harm."

"You're a fairy."

"And you look as funny as you smell," she says. "You look like a man on a mission."

"You could say that."

"A quest, even," the fairy says. "I like men on quests. They're often so much fun. Are you fun, Mr...?" She waits for him to fill in his name, but he doesn't. He sits up to see her better. She's made half of light, half of air, half of silk and lace. Her eyes are big and blue, too big and too blue for her face. "I'm a fairy," she says. "I bet I can guess your name."

"Don't," Jack says. "It's more fun that way."

She smiles. "You have a funny way of using that word. What's fun about *mystery*?" Her eyes practically sparkle when she says the word. "Oh, I see what you mean."

"What do you want?"

"Me? I can't be said to want anything, Mr. Mystery. I'm a fairy. You know what that means, right? If I want ice cream..." She snaps her fingers, and an ice cream cone appears in her hand. "I can have all the ice cream I want."

"You can't lead me astray," Jack tells her.

"Oh, you think I can't, but the truth is far simpler than that. I have already led you astray. Do you hear that?"

That, the sound means, is the caravanner stepping lightly through the woods, not more than three steps from where Jack had been sleeping. "She cannot see you, and cannot hear you." The fairy smiles. "And she dares not call your name, because she knows the value of secrets. But I know your name, don't I, Mr. Mystery? Or should I say—*DarkWalker*?"

He reaches for her, but she skips back, her wings and eyes fluttering, her smile full of teeth. "Oh, did you think I was a *good* fairy?"

He reaches forward again, stumbling through the brush, nearly knocking the caravanner down as he slips in the dead leaves at his feet. The light of dawn shines differently, in that moment, and he no longer sees the fairy.

She looks at him from above her face scarf. Her eyes are steady, narrow, and turbulent. For a moment, she doesn't say anything. Finally, she asks, "Okay?"

He nods.

"We leave in five," she tells him. "I want you at the front today. You better eat before we go."

He picks breakfast from bushes. They're the same berries the blind king had eaten when stumbling through these mountains. Had the king ruled over Babylon? Had Jack Harlow just met the very same fairy?

There's some concern in the camp. With the morning light, two of their troupe were missing. With

Jack returned, they've only lost one—but there's no trace of him. It's like he gathered all his belongings—which wouldn't have amounted to much, anyhow—taken one of the skinned animals that had been caught the night before, and disappeared sometime between the onset of night and the dawn. He'd been telling stories at the campfire. He'd insisted the mountains were home to pig men guarding a hole in the earth leading to an incomprehensible borderlands.

The caravanner goes into one of the wagons. No one enters the prisoner's wagon. The prisoner remains quiet and still. But every once in a while, if he listens, Jack Harlow hears a heart beating from within.

The caravanner stays inside with the mother for a long time. There's no telling what they discuss. No one—almost no one—knows who's really in that wagon, but no one seems willing to risk it. When she emerges, she shuts and locks the door and looks out on an expectant troupe.

"We ride," she says, and nothing more.

Jack Harlow rides near the front. The horses seem to know the way. No one walks today; everyone has made room on the horses, and the little carts have been filled to bursting with food and supplies. They stop midday for berries and fresh water from a stream. Their path dips lower, as if tempting the valley—or as if the valley tempts them—but they still travel its rim. The sky grows turbulent as clouds are gathered and trapped.

"Another storm?" Jack asks after lunch.

"No," the caravanner says. "It's just the way of the mountains."

The hawks fly closer today. The trail narrows. The peaks rise to either side, and the path is now through the valley instead of over it. It's not that the path has descended any; the mountains have grown taller and tighter.

Jack Harlow pays attention to the things he can see. The flights of hawks is but one of these things. He picks out figures in the trees, far away and deeper in the valley, of no concern except that they watch. The seers, presumably. Or more fairies. He coaxes vibrancy from threads he can feel and touch and listen to. The songs are different. The threads intersect with everyone in the caravan. They're all bound together, and with him, even those with whom he's never shared a word or a breath. Indeed, while some members of the caravan seem to be lifelong friends, few make any effort to say more than what's necessary to Jack. He understands. He keeps his distance. He keeps to himself. He keeps the silence and the shadows tight around him like coats, like skin. Some of them had been ghosts, once upon a time, and had been bent to the will of the DarkCrawler. They don't see how Jack is any different.

His secret isn't so much a secret as he'd believed. They know he's something, they just don't know what; and they're unwilling to risk being transmuted into a frog or disintegrated by a sideways thought. Some of them have probably never heard of a DarkWalker, but they see the energy vibrating under Jack's skin.

Al-Qaum, also, makes no friends. They avoid him, because his clothes reveal the tattoo on his wrist, because he's a member of one of the upper houses of Babylon, and he seems only to talk with the caravanner or with the DarkWalker.

Side by side near the front of the caravan now, Al-Qaum says, "I would love to hear a story."

"I don't know if I have a story."

"Life is merely a series of stories," Al-Qaum says. "Tell me any one of yours."

So Jack Harlow tells him about his journey into hell. "I went searching for Lisa Sparrow, but I was misled."

"You mean, lied to?"

"Essentially," Jack Harlow says. "I brought a sparrow with me into the Walled City, and the whole thing came down."

"The Prince of Thorns," Al-Qaum says, nodding. "I have heard parts of that story. He was a powerful creature, and when he was finally granted his wish—to return to earth—he was defeated by—the stories say he was defeated by the Prince of the Stable Door."

"The stories," Jack admits, "are not entirely wrong."

"You never found her."

"Not then," Jack Harlow says. "And not since. I came close. I saw her body." He takes a breath. "No, not her body. I saw a body that she'd constructed around herself—just as some of the ghosts with us now constructed their own—but she was already gone from it."

"Does it hurt, not to be with her?" Al-Qaum asks.

"It does."

"I lost my own love long ago," Al-Qaum says. "Her name was Satyanna. She was beautiful beyond measure, like the moon. She played the flute, and she sang, and she danced like a djinn, I swear it."

"What happened?"

Al-Qaum hesitates before responding. He even slows his pace, albeit subconsciously. "One day in spring, she came into these mountains."

The caravanner holds up a fist. The caravan comes quickly to a halt. Even the horses don't make any extra noises. Ahead, in the path, stands a single woman. She's elderly, and she leans on a staff. Her eyes are like storms, her skin leather, her lips cracked. After the caravan comes completely to rest, when not a muscle twitches out of place, she says, addressing the caravanner directly, "You should not bring such a prisoner into the mountains."

"I cannot leave him unattended."

The woman sneers, then turns her gaze to the other wagon. "You think you know of balance."

"It's true, I try to maintain balance," the caravanner says. "But who can say?"

The elderly woman spits once at the ground on her left. "I can say."

For a moment, a long moment, nothing more is said. Jack's got vision, sight, *something*—and he sees what flows through this woman's veins. She's looking at every member of their troupe in turn, sizing them up, reading their sins, judging them by the harshest of lights.

Finally, even after examining Jack Harlow from afar, the elderly woman says, "I make no guarantee of safety."

The caravanner nods once. Essentially, it's permission to pass, but decidedly not an offer of assistance.

The elderly woman moves aside and watches as they pass. She meets every eye as they ride by, but spits again when the prisoner's wagon draws near. She sneers at Jack Harlow but says nothing. She might give the same treatment to everyone, but the storms in her eyes recognize the storms behind his. It's uncomfortable. He doesn't like it. He doesn't like her. He doesn't even look back when they pass; he's glad just to know she's behind him.

3.

But passing the full strength of the tribe is more than just the elderly woman with the staff. Twenty minutes later, a much younger woman, perched in a tree, wears similar colors. Her eyes are milky, shot with fire, and only Jack Harlow sees her. She smiles for him, but no one else. She says something in another language, which he at first doesn't understand. But he gets it. She's telling him to be careful. To be wary. To watch out for— uncertainties. She's telling him a long climb awaits and there's no guarantee he'll survive it. She makes no promises.

An hour later, the caravan passes between a pair of women guarding either side of the path. When the caravanner reaches them, one says, "You may pass, but we will take one."

"You can't," the caravanner says. "Every member of the caravan plays an integral role."

"We will take one," the other woman says, "and you will continue on this path, deeper into the valley, until you reach the steps. There, we will decide."

The caravan continues forward. There's no sound of conflict or resistance when one of them disappears: the messenger who had ridden to meet them, to call Asteria and Jack Harlow ahead of the caravan to Babylon. He had been there, mostly quiet, often sitting with Al-Qaum but just as often sitting alone—near Anastasia's wagon.

Jack Harlow is the first to realize he's gone.

"Who was he?" Jack asks the caravanner as they walk. The path descends now, and the valley deepens, and it seems like they're marching straight down into hell.

"A brother," she says, but nothing more.

When they make camp that night, it's quieter, more subdued, and the troupe sits closer together around the bonfire. The smoke curls into the sky, sending a message to the tribe of seers and to anyone else who might catch sight of it: the caravan perseveres.

In the night, Jack Harlow hears the sound of a flutist prancing through the greenery. There are eyes in the forest, not just those of the seers. He doesn't sleep soundly, but when has he ever?

He winds the threads around his fingers. He doesn't know how they work or what they are, not exactly. He can control his vision enough to exclude the threads linking him to the caravanner (Asteria), the mother (Anastasia), the other members of the troupe. Essentially, he can diminish his awareness of those threads so that he can focus on others. So many others. Connecting him to people he knew, people who know of him, people who have died—and one of them, probably one of them—leads directly to Lisa Sparrow.

But it's not so direct as that.

Gently, almost listlessly, Jack plucks at the threads. The vibrations make notes. Every thread vibrates at a different frequency. This is the song of his life, he realizes, the song of his connections, his memories, his impacts.

"Such wonderful music," the fairy says, hopping closer, "and such beautiful colors."

"Do you want something?"

"I want many things," she says. "For now, I was just listening to you play."

"It's not music," Jack says.

"It absolutely is music."

"It's not an instrument."

"You absolutely are."

"It's—the threads that bind us," he says, lifting the one that binds him to the fairy. "We all have these."

"Oh, but those aren't so strong as you think," the fairy says, leaning on long legs to get a better view of their shared thread. She lifts the thread, ogling it like she's never seen such a thing before. "This is what keeps us together, you and me, you think?"

"It is."

The fairy produces a long-toothed pair of scissors, something direct from an Art Deco catalog, silver gleaming in the light. She snips once to show what it does. The blades are long and thin, and they sound unbelievably sharp as they cut the air. "What if I cut us free?"

She snips the thread.

And she's gone. Just like that. The thread dissipates, and starlight falls again onto the mountain pass. Jack feels something akin to a mosquito bite. It itches, briefly, where the thread had somehow connected to his hand—it's hard to say where, exactly, the threads touch him—and then even the sensation is gone. Like the fairy.

Jack Harlow tries to catch the sensation, the color, the sound of that particular thread again, but it's gone. He catches another instead, one that drifts lazily into the trees, shifting around the shadows. It's a deep indigo, so much so that it nearly burns Jack's eye to look directly at it. With a finger, he strokes the edge of the thread, and it responds with a soft cooing sound. Then, it responds more strongly, as someone on the other end of the thread releases another, different note.

And then they pluck another note.

The other end of this thread is close, and teasing him. The fairy? Possibly, but it's not at all her color or tone. This is darker, deeper, a baritone.

Unable to sleep anyway, Jack Harlow rises from his bedding and slips unseen past the caravan's watch.

The woods in the mountains are uneven and rocky, but in places the trees have broken through the rocks, creating fissures filled with the barest amount of soil.

The leaves rustle as birds and spiders and cats and other things hunt and kill.

The music of the threads gets louder and more intense as he walks. He navigates through tight passes between tall rocks, and he walks perilously close to the edge of a drop to the treetops. Once, he dislodges a small rock when he steps on it, and he listens to the thing careen down the mountainside. It bounces, cracks off the sides of the mountain and the trunks of trees, finally thumping heavily on a dirt floor too deep for Jack to see.

He's certain the fairy is shadowing his steps, giggling just beyond his range of hearing, watching from the other side of some supernatural veil he cannot see past.

That confounds him. He's a seer, among a thousand other things—by his nature as a DarkWalker—and normally he can see so much.

When he rounds a final corner in the rocks, he finds the mouth of a cave, a small fire crackling at the entrance, silence echoing from within. Seated at the fire is an old man. Frail. Thin. Leathery. The old man looks up with cataract eyes, milky and blurry.

"You were a king," Jack Harlow says. He sees it in the man's posture. He remembers it from the Al-Qaum's story.

The man laughs and coughs, briefly, and waves down at the ground around the fire. "Sit, sit."

Jack Harlow sits across the fire from the old man, who offers a battered bowl full of berries. "Eat, eat," he says.

"Thank you, no."

"More for me," the man says, pouring a handful straight into his mouth. He chews loudly. Berry juice spills from the corners of his mouth like blood. Then he tosses the metal bowl aside and sighs deeply.

The threads never get loose and never seem to tighten. The one connecting him to this man—this king?—is thin and no longer very long. It bows across the fire, unaffected by the flames. Jack plucks a note from it.

The king smiles, closes his eyes and enjoys it, then reaches for the very same thread. "You would steal my story," the king says suddenly.

"What?"

"You're a thief," the king says, "and should be executed. To the gallows with you!"

There is no one to respond to his command.

Jack merely looks across the fire at him. The thread between them trembles. The sound is disharmonious and in a minor key.

The king grabs a fistful of berries and shoves them into his mouth. He bends his head all the way back as though looking to the sky. From this deep in the mountains, the sky is extraordinarily clear, like a piece of black crystal dotted with jewels. "Have they executed you yet?"

Jack Harlow glances around. There's no one in the cavern, no one on the little path, no one in the trees, and no one in the sky. He says, "No."

"Good," the king says. "I didn't mean it anyway." He leans forward, nearer to the fire, and says, "Sometimes, they take me seriously, and they do what I say, and even I—yes—even I can admit they scare me." He lowers his voice to barely a whisper. "And they should scare you, too."

"I don't scare easily," Jack Harlow says. It's not boasting. Indeed, it's half lamentation. He wishes he could be scared again. The night has never held secrets from him.

The king picks up the bowl again to scoop out the last of the berries. "I didn't used to, either," he says, tossing the bowl aside. He plucks at the string between them. "What is it, then, that connects us?"

"I don't know."

The king smiles. It's a smile that's missing some teeth. It's dusty, even in the lush valley, and for a moment the clouds in his eyes seem to at least consider parting. He lifts the edge of their indigo thread and says, "This is the only thing I can see anymore. This, and other things like it, ethereal things, insubstantial things, unreal things. Do you want to know what that's like?"

Jack Harlow doesn't answer. It feels like a rhetorical question, but the answer is no. He never asked for any of these so-called gifts.

The king hisses, his teeth suddenly too many needles in a rounded mouth, the clouds in his eyes now filled with thunder. He lunges at Jack, swiping at him with a bone-thin arm, smacking him softly on the cheek.

"Oh, hell," the king says, settling back to sitting and staring—unseeingly—at his own hand in front of his face. "Used to be, I had claws, I had talons, I could rip craters out of the moon." He flexes the fingers, tightens them into a ball, flexes them again. "Are you here to rescue me?"

"Do you need rescuing?" Jack asks.

"I need things," the king says. "Isn't that enough?"

"We're travelling deeper, and further, and you're maybe safer here, to be honest," Jack tells him. The old man frowns, and it's the deepest, saddest thing Jack's ever seen. "You can come with us," he adds, "but we're going to other realms."

"I was born in other realms," the king says, hopping to his feet. "Let me just get my things, all my things, did you see where I put my bowl? I need my bowl. And..." The old man leans down, snatches the bowl from the ground, then kicks dirt onto his little fire. "Used to be, I ate something other than berries." He smashes the bowl against the mouth of the cave. But it's metallic, if cheap and thin. It doesn't break or shatter, merely rings atonally. "We're connected, you and I, aren't we?" He pulls on the thread. Jack feels a physical tugging.

"I suppose we are."

"Oh, it's good to know," the king says. "So few threads remain unbroken. Once they start, you should know, once they start ripping or tearing or cutting, all the threads, all your connections, will get unstable, and will break, and will leave you afloat in a sea of nothingness." Then he smiles, holding up his bowl and a handkerchief he's just pulled from a pocket, and says, "I'm ready to go."

Quietly and quickly, Jack Harlow extinguishes the fire. The dirt the old man had kicked into it hadn't had any real affect. "Used to be," the king says, "I was a king."

The king follows Jack Harlow back through the woods. He's just retracing the same steps he'd taken, but Jack already knows the caravan won't be there. The quality of the light has changed. The quantity. The thickness of it. Somewhere nearby, the fairy's giggling, and Jack realizes he never should have left their camp. The thread to this rambling old man had been created by the fairy, a means for leading him astray.

At the next turn in his path, however, Jack finds himself—he and the king—surrounded. A dozen women, all their eyes on him, all their eyes unique. One set of eyes glows, another draws breath, another crackles with infant lightning. The women range in age from seven to maybe a hundred and seven. Not a single one smiles.

"Oh, that's right," the king says. "Used to be, I was free to be rescued, but I forget sometimes—I'm old, you see—I forget that I can't escape, and all I can eat any more is berries, because they got tired of me eating people." He thrusts out the empty bowl. "And hey, look at that, I'm all out of berries."

One—only one—of the women steps forward, and only one step. It's a forceful step, and the king hops back—like a jester, not a king at all. He hops once, his legs all akimbo, then races back the way they came, toward the mouth of his cave, abandoning Jack Harlow to the tribe of seers.

She turns her honey-colored eyes on Jack and speaks with a honey-coated voice. "You shouldn't wander."

Jack Harlow nods. He's not quite sure it's advice he can ever follow. All his life has been wandering. He says, "I don't know what else to do."

The seers all blink as one. It's a slow, deliberate blink. It feels hostile, or at least invasive, maybe threatening. There's no place to step back to, as they're all around him now, and there's twice as many as he'd noticed just a moment ago.

"Stay on the path," the seer tells him, "and stay with your guide, and don't stray again, Jack Harlow, lest you want to become lost."

CHAPTER THREE

1.

In the morning, the caravan continues deeper into the valley. The descent is steep. The wagons are watched carefully. The mother never emerges from hers, the prisoner never makes a sound. "What if he's not in there anymore?" Jack asks the caravanner.

"It can't happen," she says.

"When did you last hear anything from him? Or feed him?"

"He goes silent for years at a time," she says. "He eats when he wants to. I have nothing to do with it."

They're rounding a curve in a side of the mountain so deep, they cannot see the peek. The path is only wide enough for one wagon, but they have to take it slowly lest it roll out of control down the path or slip a wheel over the side and tumble straight to the unseen bottom.

"What if the seers took him, when they said they'd take one?" Jack asks. The seers had left him alone in the blink of an eye; he'd reached the caravan's campsite just as dawn was breaking.

She shakes her head. She doesn't believe it, can't even imagine it; and if she revealed the identity of the prisoner to Jack, he'd probably understand. He sees all this in her eyes, but she's no longer looking at him. She's looking ahead, at the end of the path, at the bottom of this descent, at the foot of a staircase a thousand steps high.

The steps double back over each other. They're narrow and they're broken. There are switchbacks, sections that seem to defy gravity and physics; and at a dizzying height, the stairs disappear into the side of the mountain.

A group of the seers stand at the foot of the stairs. Half of them have blindfolds over their eyes. One of the younger women approaches the caravanner. "You'll find your friend inside," she says. "It's a long climb, but it's straight." The seer turns her attention to Jack Harlow, but still speaks to the caravanner. "I would give you advice."

"I wouldn't take it," the caravanner says.

The seer nods, and steps aside. The others step away from the bottom of the stairs. They're steep, and the two wagons will not easily make the climb. The caravanner knocks on the door to the mother's wagon, waits a moment for a response, then unlocks the door and lets herself in. The rest of the caravan keep their distance. Jack hears the prisoner laughing. It's short-lived, but it's there; and for some reason, this brings him some relief.

When the caravanner emerges from the wagon, she's not alone. Anastasia, wrapped from head to toe in silken scarves, the epitome of grace even when completely covered, follows. She goes to the prisoner's wagon, circles it three times counterclockwise, reciting ancient poetics. Jack can see the intricacies of the magic being worked, the underlying sparks, the glamour, the mechanizations. She folds the wagon in on itself, and again, and again, until it's reduced to the size of a soccer ball.

It's no less heavy than it was, and it takes four of their troupe, using a makeshift stretcher of wood and cloth, to carry it. The wagon will slow their ascent but not prevent it.

The other carts, they abandon with the mother's wagon. The horses hesitate before taking the first step. They don't outright refuse, but they have to be coaxed into making the climb. Two of the troupe whisper with the horses. The caravanner and her mother stand off to one side, sharing secrets even Jack Harlow's ears cannot pick off the wind.

Al-Qaum stands with Jack. Together, they stare into the clouds, into which the height of this mountain vanishes. "That's a long climb," Al-Qaum says, "and one rarely made. You know what's inside?"

"No."

"Stories," Al-Qaum says. "And some of those tales, after all this, will have us at the center of them." He looks as excited as a schoolboy going on his first trick-or-treat.

The ascent is slow. At the bottom, the steps are even and regular enough. But they're steep, right from the start, and grow steeper as they climb. Carved from the natural rock, the steps are ragged and jagged and, as they rise, unstable. More than once, a bad step sends pebbles tumbling over the edge.

In places, the stairs are wide, but mostly they're too narrow for two people to walk side by side. The horses seem perfectly fine, but some members of the caravan, perhaps more used to the desert, stumble occasionally and hug the mountainside even in places where it's not necessary.

Jack Harlow climbs near the rear, Al-Qaum just ahead of him, while the caravanner and the mother lead the party.

Between steps, in places, there are inclines, ramps, and even declines, as though whoever had built these stairs had been forced to follow the geography of the mountain rather than vice versa. For some reason, that brings Jack Harlow some comfort. It implies the foundations of the staircase, the architecture of it all, is solid.

The climb is intense. Several times, for different people, they're forced to stop. Jack Harlow feels the burn of climbing in his muscles, but he maintains more strength than he might have thought. He doesn't need to stop, but he's thankful each time. At one point, they stop close to a trickle of water on the furthest side of the stairs so they can drink. Their crisscross path confounds the mountain goats watching from the safety of impossible outcroppings no one else could use. Birds, hawks primarily, circle close, but never close enough to put themselves in danger. Not that anyone in the troupe would snatch one. The birds don't know the range of someone like Jack Harlow.

They rotate people through the task of carrying the prisoner's shrunken wagon. It's tough work, and even Jack Harlow, when it's his turn, suffers under that weight. He hadn't imagined. It's quite the burden. Indeed, it seems more a burden for him than anyone else. And his is the strength of the DarkWalker. His is the impossible, unknowable, untested strength of what might have been a god.

When they rest at the end of his turn carrying the burden, it's nearly dusk. The light has changed again, so it's stretched thinner, so that the twilight—in this twilight place—seems at risk of breaking. They're near enough that trickle of water to send the acrobat—Jack hadn't even realized there was an acrobat—to collect water in small jugs. They let Jack Harlow drink first.

Then he falls asleep. Deeply. Thoroughly. All the way to his bones.

It's night, or near enough night that they ought to rest, though the stairs provide few natural places for it. Jack Harlow doesn't dream, except to see the side of the mountain, the steps, the fall should he go over the edge. It's a long way down. At the base of these mountain stairs, three dozen of the seers have gathered around a fire. At random intervals, one or more of them turn their eyes upwards, golden eyes and silver eyes, clouded eyes, blank eyes, eyes of inescapable obsidian.

When he looks back, when he meets the eyes of any one, they avert their gaze.

In the distance, behind them, not part of their circle at the fire, the old king eats berries, his chin stained with their red juice. He looks up the side of the mountain and grins. Sometimes, that grin is missing teeth. Sometimes, it's all needles. Sometimes, it's a bottomless drop into the back of his throat.

When Jack Harlow wakes, the rest of the troupe sleeps. Surely, someone has remained awake to keep watch, but Jack cannot see them.

He half expects to find the fairy, perched on a ledge too small to support her wriggling fingers at him, but no one's visible. It's a dawning moment, the very end of the night, which surprises Jack Harlow and makes him wonder if perhaps he's still asleep, dreaming, drifting through layers of consciousness.

The wind carries the scent of distant thunderstorms.

Jack Harlow picks his way up the stairs, around the sleeping troupe, past the horses who seem displeased by his nearness, until he reaches the place where the caravanner and the mother sleep.

"You should rest better," Anastasia, the mother, says without opening her eyes.

"I should, but I don't."

"Are we following the paths of your threads?"

The threads have retreated into the background of Jack's periphery, but they're never so far away that he can't reach out and wring a note from one. "Not precisely."

"It's the mountains," she tells him. "Moving on the third axis will confound them. You'll see better, I'm sure, when we reach the top."

"How long?" Jack asks.

She opens her eyes, shields them from the first rays of sunlight, and says, "It looks a long way."

"It's a long way down, too," Jack tells her.

"Ever the optimist, aren't you?" She smiles as she

asks it. "There's more below than above, but then we enter the mountain, and that's when we truly begin our ascent."

"Aren't there other paths?" Jack asks.

"You know the value of the journey. If you try to transport to the place you need to go—if you even know where that is—the act of transportation alters the value of the destination. This path, this arduous path, this physical path, makes it more important."

"And the caravan?" Jack asks. "I get the impression you and I could do this trip on our own."

She shakes her head slowly. Kindly, even.

The caravanner, having awoken, says, "We go our own way, Jack Harlow, just as you. For the moment, our paths are the same. Enjoy that while you can, because there will come a time when we must face ourselves on our own."

The sound of her voice, if not the words, drifts down the stairs, gently rousing the rest of the troupe, even those who had not been completely asleep.

From here, the stairs become less steady, less structured, less reliable. There are places where the stairs have crumbled, forcing them to maneuver over rubble. When the smallest of rocks falls off the side, it bounces and bounces, bounces again, and eventually disappears. They never hear it reach bottom. The top of the mountain remains in the clouds. In the morning, the sun reaches under those clouds from far in the east. But as it rises, the day darkens, and the clouds grow thicker, darker, colder.

It's still early in the day when they pass above the tree line. The hawks blend better with the rocky side of the mountain. There's still vegetation, but it's mostly rough, brownish shrubbery that blends with the colors of the rocks.

Other things blend with the rocks, things that watch,

that follow, that track and stalk. They're not all night things, not all creatures of darkness, and none are necessarily evil. Jack Harlow doesn't take notice of them until well into their second day of ascending. Past noon, when they stop for a brief reset and meal, one of the long, stringy birds gets brave enough to come close. It darts in, seemingly going for the food, but at that last minute changes its trajectory and flies at Al-Qaum's face.

Just as Al-Qaum becomes aware of the bird, Jack catches it by the neck. The bird squawks. Its beak is a razor, its talons oversized, its eyes pink like taffy. It flaps its wings, it writhes in Jack's hands—and its brethren swoop in.

The flock attacks, almost immediately driving one of the horses over the side of the stairs. One of the troupe goes with it.

Anastasia whistles.

It starts as a low sound, increasing in both pitch and volume. Anastasia rises to her full height—she seems to nearly double in size—and with only a brief breath, changes the nature of the whistle. At first, the birds scatter, but they don't go far. They glide around the side of the stairs as though there's an invisible barrier they can't cross.

Then one of the hawks attacks. It smashes one of the long-necked white birds in midair. They plunge together, the hawk's beak already tearing into the flesh. A second hawk attacks, and finally the other birds flee. Some are chased. Anastasia brings her whistling song—it was hardly a song, but not merely a single note—to an end. Silence drops over them. The only white bird still visible is the one in Jack's hand. He had crushed its throat without realizing it. Now, seeing this thing in his hand, this thing so much like birds he's seen, he tosses it down the side of the mountain.

"Thanks," Al-Qaum says.

"Just birds," Jack says.

Al-Qaum shakes his head. "Harvesters," he says. "It would've taken my soul to a realm of shadows."

Jack looks down the side of the mountain. "We lost someone."

Al-Qaum nods. "If he's fortunate, he merely died."

Jack Harlow runs his fingers through the threads that connect him to everyone. They're insubstantial, even invisible, until he touches them, and even then they're barely present. He doesn't recognize who each thread is associated with. There's the one that leads back to the king in the valley, but that's the only one he knows.

That can't be right.

Al-Qaum puts a hand on Jack's arm. "Some mysteries are not meant to be known."

The caravanner announces, "We should move. There are other, worse predators in the mountains. Let's move, double time, until we can get safely inside the mountain. I don't want to lose anyone else on the way, have you got that? Now move!"

The caravan gathers itself more quickly than usual, tying down everything that can be to the backs of all but one of the remaining horses. The prisoner's wagon is bound to the last, tied up in a different kind of stretcher, secured, and dragged that way. The horse that had fallen, everyone realizes, had held half their food.

However, double time at this point is close to the same progress they'd already been making. They reach a broken spot in the stairs, where erosion or sabotage has completely wiped away about ten steps. It's a long length and a high jump. The acrobat makes the jump first, showing that it can be done. The mother goes next. Then the horses, one at a time. Their loads need to be removed before they can be enticed to make the jump.

Jack doesn't want to watch, but the horses—four of them now—all make the leap.

Then it's the rest of the troupe. Five of them before Al-Qaum's turn, leaving only Jack and the caravanner on the lower side. Only one of them has any trouble, but he's caught by the others before he can slip backwards and plummet to his death.

"Should be easy for you," the caravanner says.

Jack Harlow smiles. He's not a man who smiles often, but it feels sincere. There's nothing sarcastic or wicked about it. It's a genuine expression of—of something good—and he's not used to it.

She winks. "I'll leave you to think about it." She makes the jump with excessive ease, enough to even put the acrobat to shame. Jack takes a breath—he almost doesn't need it—and starts his jump. It's a two-step running start, and then the jump—but he gets tangled in the threads, the insubstantial threads, the invisible binds to people far and away.

He's caught, briefly, in their spider web between one side and the other. Over the chasm. It might be twenty or thirty feet before he bounces on the set of stairs below them and then off the side of the mountain. He doesn't know if he'd survive the fall.

But he's stuck. In midair. He pushes forward, reaches for the caravanner on the other side, and a dozen or two dozen of the threads come apart.

He slips downward. The threads, the dozens that remain, pull him down. He resists. He trembles.

The acrobat and the caravanner move quickly. She climbs onto the acrobat's thighs as he leans back. Others hold the acrobat. Creating a V between them, the caravanner can reach further toward Jack Harlow. Her reach is just a little shy.

"More," she says to the acrobat.

He's right at the edge. Pebbles and clumps of dirt

dribble from beneath the soles of his feet. His toes are over the edge. Four people hold him. Anastasia looks on from several steps up, the concern on her face a mask beneath the scarves. Jack still sees it, and it makes him nervous.

He reaches further. His fingertips brush the caravanner's. Still not close enough for one to grasp the other. More threads rip. The sound is jarring, like slamming a fist on the center of an out-of-tune piano's keyboard. Blood drips wetly from his ears and nose. He strains further, harder, tearing more of the threads, so that he can curl his finger around the caravanner's. It's not enough to pull a person, but maybe it's enough to hold onto.

The threads yank him back.

He slips, and this time he's dislodged from whatever force holds him in the air. He tries to hold onto her finger, but it's not enough of a fulcrum.

Jack Harlow falls.

He crashes onto the stairs below. He tumbles down, head over heels—down the stairs, not down off the side of the mountain. He's able to control his fall enough to prevent that. He smashes into the rocks and finally comes to a halt. He's only—perhaps—three stories down.

He also feels weak, weak in a way he hasn't been before. Not since he was a teenager, a child, an infant. The brief but overwhelming sensation fades with the sound of the splintered threads. They dangle from him like open wounds. They bleed wisps of color that dissipate into the air.

He checks himself over. Nothing broken. He bleeds actual blood from a few good scrapes and cuts, but not dangerous amounts. It's nothing serious. His ankles work, his legs work, and he takes almost no time at all to get them under him again.

But when he does, Anastasia is there, directly in front of him, arms around his shoulders to help keep him steady. "I don't know what happened," he admits. The rest of the caravan has already continued to climb. He wonders how long he must've been unconscious for so much to have changed.

"You're unhurt," Anastasia says, "just shaken."

"I misunderstood something," Jack says.

She smiles. It amazes him, that he can sense the smile through the scarves. It touches her eyes, but it's more than that. The fabric shifts. He can almost see the curve of her mouth. Briefly, he reaches up to touch her lips through the fabric. She allows this. He realizes quite quickly what he's doing and pulls back.

"You're going through a lot," Anastasia says. "The stresses on your body—you're primarily human, underneath all the rest of it. You were never meant for what you're going through."

"What is it I'm going through?"

She shrugs, and begins to guide him back up the stairs. "Metamorphosis."

2.

Anastasia walks with Jack up the steps. It doesn't take long to get back to where he fell. The crevice seems bigger now. He doesn't even have to ask the question. She says, "You broke parts of it when you fell, though you never touched it."

"How do I know it won't happen again?" Jack asks.

"This is a lesson, then," Anastasia tells him. "In trust."

"Do I trust you, is that it?" Jack asks. "I do."

She shakes her head. "Do you trust yourself?"

That's a tough question. He doesn't know. He's never considered it. The weight of it lands heavily on his shoulders, on his head. His vision clouds—albeit briefly—but long enough to raise doubts.

"Your power, your strength, your abilities," Anastasia says, "accelerated so quickly, you didn't even know what you were capable of. Now, they've diminished again, but not to the boy you were at seventeen. You have strength, you have hidden talents, and you have the one thing that's most important in all the realms."

He narrows his eyes. "Love?"

She smiles. "You're getting it."

"No," Jack says, "I'm not."

"What drives you? Why are you on this journey? You're not seeking power anymore, or revenge, or anything other than to be with the woman you love. That gives you focus, and that gives you strength. I believe in your strength, Jack Harlow, DarkWalker, Destroyer of Hells. Do you?"

"It wasn't a lack of belief that got me stuck," he says.

"Maybe not." She smiles again. As she does so, the sky cracks open—an arc of lightning splits it. The boom of thunder shakes the mountain. And the rain comes down like a waterfall.

Anastasia tilts her head to look up. She opens her mouth, spreads her hands, and doesn't even look ahead of her as she leaps over the break in the steps. She doesn't jump so much as glide, and lands without a hint of unbalance on the other side. Jack doesn't take the two steps this time. He simply launches.

Tattered threads fly out behind him as he does.

He lands effortlessly beside Anastasia. She smiles again.

It's another seven or eight switchbacks, slippery now because of the rain, before they reach the stop of the stairs. They end at an arched entryway leading into the mountain. Crossing the threshold, they find more stairs circling the interior of the mountain and rising toward what appears to be a break in the top. Rain drops into the mountain within the circle of stairs, sounding like a massive series of waterfalls the size of Niagara. Thunder booms and rumbles echo and magnify within the stairs.

Looking out across the stairs—he cannot see the bottom, where the rain ultimately falls, though he hears it—the stairway curls at a relatively steady rate. The walls to the interior of the mountain are arched bricks, gold and crimson; the outer walls are the natural sides of the mountain.

"It's a long climb," Anastasia says. "Are you ready for what we'll find at the top?"

"I have no idea what we'll find."

"Neither do I. This is a lesson for me, as well. I've never left Babylon before."

3.

The caravan has circled the insides of the mountain about ten times before Anastasia and Jack, not hurrying, catch up to them. The steps are wider inside, and better kept. A lot of light comes down from the top of the mountain, but there are also torches at intervals. Someone keeps those fires burning. Their sounds—their feet, the horses, the dragging of the miniaturized wagon—echo through the mountain. They do not travel with stealth.

They make camp. Only Jack Harlow and Anastasia were caught in the rain, so they sit close to the fire when they light it. Food and wine is passed around. The general mood of the caravan seems good; they're singing and telling stories. When it's Al-Qaum's turn to spin a tale, he talks about ancient gods traveling through the desert in search of a carnival troupe. Everyone seems to know the story but Jack. They point out when Al-Qaum makes mistakes, they laugh together, they add side-stories to do with jaguars and frogs.

Anastasia says to Jack, "There will be repercussions."

"The broken threads?"

"Can you read them yet?"

"I've gotten—maybe hints," Jack frowns. When the wine bottle is passed to him, he hands it off to the next person without taking a swallow. "Suggestions. Possibilities. The king, for instance."

She shakes her head. "We don't talk much about kings."

"It was just a story."

She pokes a stick into the fire, glances up into the shaft. Rain still falls in a torrent. "It's interesting, don't you think?"

"That I would hear of the king, then meet him so quickly?"

"That, too."

Jack shakes his head. "But I learned nothing from the king."

"Yet, I can see it, the trace of it, the indigo," Anastasia says. "You're still connected to a king you know nothing about, except a story told near a fire during a valley excursion."

"You don't trust the stories?" Jack asks.

"I don't trust the valley."

It's Jack's turn to smile. "We were just talking about trust."

"It's one thing to trust yourself," Anastasia says, turning her eyes—twin suns—on him. There's no sign of humor. She does not smile. "You hear stories of the twilight places, though, and you meet people, and you begin to realize trust shouldn't always be an automatic thing. The seers in the valley, do you know for certain we're done with them? Do you think we're safe, inside this mountain?" She adds his name silently; it wouldn't be good to let such a secret loose inside an echo chamber. "You have good eyes, and you use them well. Don't let them rest, not here, maybe not ever. Most of the world is not divided into the dark and the light. Most of the world, those things are interconnected, entwined together, like in the twilight places. Like in your soul." Again, she would say his name. He hears it in her tone.

Night passes quickly. It's still strange, for Jack Harlow, to sleep by night and travel by day. For so many years, the night kept him awake, kept him wandering, searching for some place where he could escape all the things in the dark. Vampires, ghosts, and shades haunted his every turn. He rests, but doesn't exactly sleep. Overnight, the rain slows, even inside the mountain, so the caravan wakes to an explosion of golden light from above. It bounces off random water drops and throws rainbows in every direction.

Anastasia, through the scarves on her face, gives Jack Harlow a smile, then without a word continues the circling trek upwards.

Partway up, they find a fountain on the outer part of the mountain wall. It must be thicker here, deeper into the mountain. It's a small pool with translucent fish swimming around the statue of a woman with a fish in her hand, a spout in the fish's mouth spills water into one side of the little pool.

Despite the fish, they do not drink. Instead, the caravanner leaves something—Jack Harlow doesn't know what—she drops it gently into the pool and says something to the statue. He knows or recognizes a dozen languages, maybe more, but not the words she uses. It's a prayer of some sort.

"Who is that?" Jack asks Al-Qaum.

"That is a statue, and not a person. Are you feeling okay? Have you got a fever?"

"Why does she leave a gift?"

"Sometimes, on the paths we take, we find places of worship that do not belong to us. Even then, we should be reverent, don't you think? It's not every day we run the risk of offending gods."

"I believe I've offended my fair share."

Al-Qaum smiles at him. "From the stories I've heard, more than a fair share."

"I'm not sure all these stories are true."

"They may not be accurate," Al-Qaum says, "but they are most certainly true."

As he passes the statue, Jack watches its eyes. They're stone. They don't seem to move to follow him but he still feels as though he's being watched.

They are being watched. Not just him. And while it may be because he's traveling with the caravan, there may be any number of other reasons for someone to watch them. This may be someone's territory.

A short while after the statue, they find the horseman the seers had snatched. He sits on a bare wood chair. He leans forward and holds his head in his hands. He rocks gently. At first, he doesn't acknowledge the caravan's approach. Finally, when they're too close to ignore, he lifts his head to look at them.

His eyes are gone. His tears are blood.

The caravanner rushes to his side. "What happened?"

He shakes his head. "I don't remember."

"You can tell me."

"I can't."

"You're safe with us."

"I'm not."

He doesn't sound at all like the horseman who had met them in the desert. Gone are all shades of confidence and control. He's been broken, not just in the eyes.

Al-Qaum says to Jack, "The seers always exact a price."

"Is it always eyes?"

"No."

"The things I've seen," the horseman says, shaking his head.

The caravanner looks to Anastasia, but receives only a slight shake of the head. She turns back to the horseman, putting hands on his shoulders, helping him to his feet. "How long have you been here?"

"Forever."

"That's not true."

"The things I've seen..." He shakes his head wildly; his whole body follows with it. "I can't unsee them. They're burned into my brain. Imprinted. The horror..." He turns his head toward Jack Harlow, near the back of the caravan, and says, "They're watching you, Jack Harlow."

The echo of his name ripples through the other members of the caravan just as it echoes up and down the interior of the mountain.

"There's no hiding anymore," the horseman says. "It'll all be out in the open. *Exposed*. And you will suffer for it, for the things you've done, for the evils you let loose."

Anastasia steps forward and lays her soft hand on his shoulder. "Shush, now, child," she says. "You're rambling."

He shakes his head again. "I'm telling truths."

"You're revealing *secrets*," Anastasia says. "What have I taught you?" He doesn't answer, doesn't even try; whatever she taught, revealing secrets is the opposite of it. "Does it hurt, Alexis?"

He gives his head a little shake. "There's only pain, now."

"Come, relax a moment, let your mother help." She leads him back, down the stairs, toward the back of the caravan. No one moves except to watch. The horseman trembles as he walks, and would fall if not for Anastasia's support. As they reach Jack Harlow, who also only watches, she says, "Come with me, please."

Jack Harlow stands on the other side of Alexis; together, they walk him down the steps, eventually reaching the statue and the little pool around it. The caravan, meanwhile, continues moving forward; there's no reason to wait.

They sit Alexis on the step nearest the pool. Anastasia splashes some water in his face. She doesn't bother to thank the represented goddess. Alexis writhes in pain when the water gets in his eye sockets.

"Hold him down," she orders.

Jack Harlow pins Alexis's arms to his side,

whispers, "You'll be okay."

Briefly, Alexis smiles. "I will be. Will you?"

Then the pain returns, and he writhes again, like a snake in a trap, like an infant godling in a cage.

Anastasia looks at Jack. Slowly, deliberately, she removes enough of her face scarves to fully reveal her smile. It's radiant, almost too bright to handle. "I am not a healer."

For a moment, Jack doesn't know what to do. When he realizes what she means, he says, "Oh."

"There are stories," she says.

"That was another version of me."

"No." She shakes her head. She touches his hand. "It's all still within you."

Jack Harlow nods. He believes her. He doesn't know why. He's never really been much for believing in a person before—not until or since Lisa Sparrow. He's kept people close, but always sensed some level of duplicity. Ulterior motives. Wicked intentions. With Anastasia, he senses none of that; it may be that all of his powers have diminished. Or she hides her truths more effectively than anyone else.

Jack casts those thoughts from his mind. He focuses on the horseman. He says, "The last time I tried to heal someone, I healed her—too thoroughly. Too forcefully. She'd been a three thousand year old vampire, and I made her human again."

Anastasia nods once. "That's not the story I heard."

Jack inhales. Jia Li, who had once fought with him against the onslaught of night, who had nearly given her life to protect him, had suffered a grave injustice at his hands. Just one of many, many such people. But for her—because of the nature of her talents—not exclusively because of that—he cares about her, loves her even, in a way. He doesn't know what happened to her after he died.

He releases his breath. One of the tattered crimson threads had led to her. They're no longer connected. It saddens him.

Another inhalation. He looks into the eyes—into the ragged, bloody sockets—of the horseman. Alexis. The way the eyes were removed: violent, without regard to what may happen after. Infection burns through raw optic nerves. But they weren't removed just physically. There's no way to restore his eyesight. His eyes have been replaced with the seeds of a seer's eyes. His vision will never be the same.

But Jack can numb the pain. It takes only a little effort. He's afraid to try restructuring anything at an atomic level; once before, he was able to do that, but he'd been intoxicated with power and believed he could do no wrong. He knows better now.

He removes Alexis's pain. Anastasia douses his eyes again with water from the fountain.

"How is it now?" she asks.

"Better." He hesitates. "I can't see, mother."

"You'll never see again," Jack tells him. "Not in the way you're used to. But eyes will..." He pauses, unsure of the correct word. He was never a wordsmith. "Eyes will grow again in your head. For now, we just need to keep them clean and dry."

He reaches further into Alexis's head—not physically—to eradicate all traces of infection. Then Anastasia uses a handful of her face scarves to create a blindfold. She wraps it carefully around his eyes.

"I would be lying if I claimed this was for your benefit," she says, "but there are some who won't understand, some even in your sister's caravan."

"Won't understand what?" Alexis asks.

"The things you're going to understand, in time. For now, just relax, and try not to think about anything, and try not to focus on the things you can see."

Alexis nods. Jack releases his arms, leans back, sighs heavily.

"That took effort, didn't it?" Anastasia asks.

"It did."

"You're beginning to recognize your true self," Anastasia says, "beneath all the stories, beneath the lies you've told yourself, beneath the myths and legends."

"There's things you're not telling me," he says.

"It's true." She touches her stomach briefly. It's still flat, but there are two threads connecting the two of them. "I've never been pregnant before."

"They all call you mother."

"It's an honor," she says, "and a truth, but it's not accurate."

"And now?"

"Our child," she says, "will likely be something that's never existed before. You are a DarkWalker, I am—what I am."

"What are you, exactly? Why don't I know?"

"I'm a creature of the light now," she says. "I exist in the places you cannot see."

"That's not an answer."

"I am, in essence, the opposite of you. A LightWalker, you might say, though there's no real name for what I am. I am the first and only of my kind."

"I'm not the first DarkWalker."

"You're the seventh," she says. Then: "I know a great many things." She still doesn't give voice to his name, though Alexis seems to bristle at the exclusion. "But we have created something different."

"That wasn't my intention," he says.

"It was mine, though."

Jack Harlow was never a father and never wanted to be one. He doesn't know what to do with that information. His own father—well, there's still a question there. Was his father his father? He doesn't know. The man lied about it, lied about much, had used and manipulated Jack Harlow and his sister, and in the end was hanged for his relationship with Jack.

They sit for a while. Alexis says nothing, but rocks gently, hugging his knees, head turned as though he's looking at something. Eventually, he says, "I think I'm ready."

They climb the stairs, following the path of the caravan. They step around fresh manure. Alexis conducts himself as though he can see. His other senses are compensating. His vision, whatever it will become, has already started to take shape. The blindfold won't prevent him from seeing in his new way.

Night arrives. The golden shaft of light plummeting through the center of the stairway vanishes suddenly, leaving only the scattered torches.

"We should rest here," Anastasia says.

"We should catch up to the caravan," Jack says.

"In the dark?"

"None of us needs the light to see," Jack points out.

"You're not entirely right."

"If they get too far ahead of us, we'll never catch up."

"If we travel through the dark, we'll never be able to defend ourselves."

Jack Harlow considers that. Alexis, being blind, may be defenseless. Anastasia, a self-proclaimed creature of the light, may be without defense in the dark. But this is Jack's time, the only time he's really lived in since the night of his seventeenth birthday, since that ghost kissed him in the basement. A lifetime ago. Several lifetimes. How many times has Jack Harlow died? He's dead now, dead and gone from the earth, crossing other realms as something other than a spirit— even after his spirit was destroyed. Does he persist still because he is a DarkWalker, or do all people continue their lives in other realms?

"I went looking for Lisa once," Jack says, beginning a story, sitting on the edge of the step and perhaps conceding that they should rest for the night. "I went through a variety of hells."

"You don't stink of the hellish realms," Anastasia says.

"But I can see them," Alexis says suddenly, pointing. "Your aura, Jack..." He pauses, and doesn't complete Jack's name. "The hellish realms are shot through the color of you, the very essence of you, like veins in an opal. I want to say tainted, but that's not right."

"Of course it's not," Anastasia says. "They're a part of you, all things you've seen and done are a part of you. Alexis, what else do you see in his aura?"

Alexis takes a short breath. He doesn't want to answer. "Death."

"What does that mean?" Jack asks.

"I see the faces of those you've killed," Alexis says. "And many of them are wicked, distorted faces, and they have no true substance. But some are human. Some are innocent. You've killed, even when you weren't meaning to. But I see most clearly those you killed who did not deserve it."

"I see their faces, too."

"And I see those who have died around you, or because of you, rather than at your hand. Defending you. Fighting for you. Trying to help." He lowers his voice. "And I see shadows. The shadows that followed you through the desert. They're still with you."

Jack nods. "Debts must be paid."

But Alexis shakes his head. "I see anger, too, and frustration, and things I don't understand. But I'm beginning to."

"That's enough for now," Anastasia says. "We don't want to give our friend nightmares."

Alexis laughs or coughs or something. He says, "I will never have anything but nightmares. But there's something more, something important. I'm not sure what it is. But you can see the threads that bind you to others, right? The connections? I know you can. You're looking at them now. The one that leads to me is weak. Two lead to mother, you know that. But there's another, a strong one, leading to the top of this mountain. I don't know who waits for you up there, but you are awaited."

CHAPTER FOUR

1.

Jack Harlow does not sleep. He rests, if leaning against the wall with one eye and ear always paying attention counts as rest. He doesn't even approach sleep. It's a foreign concept to him now. He doesn't feel tired at all.

Anastasia sleeps. Her face is exposed now, and the rhythm of her breathing is intoxicating. He can watch her all night, but he still wishes she was Lisa.

They had so brief a time. But she'd touched something inside him, something beyond the physical. She'd made him believe in hope. Love. Possibility. With her, he'd believed he might escape his life of wandering the nights. He might be able to ignore the things he saw. In the beginning, that's all it was. He saw the ghouls. The monsters. He didn't realize he was becoming one, absorbing bits of them into himself, becoming more and more like the creatures he thought he was supposed to watch.

After Lisa, after she died protecting him, after she died saving his life, he didn't know if he wanted to live. He didn't want to die, necessarily, but he'd wandered with his own broken soul for a while, drank whatever he could steal, and eventually was set on a course by—well, a god—that ultimately led him here. None of this—the journeys into hells, the Thorny Prince, the Shallow and Deep Cities, the Susquehanna Incident, everything that happened in the New York City brownstone, and then Shangri La, Armageddon, and finally the DarkCrawler— none of it would have happened if he'd been able to save Lisa Sparrow that night in Orlando from a self-inflicted wound to rid herself of the demon that she'd allowed to possess her in order to save him.

She had been brave, strong, maybe a little foolish— and he'd been very much so, he should have known better, he'd been a bad watcher. He'd never really known anything. Even now, he's all questions—and since meeting Anastasia, all wonder.

Wonder is a new thing for him. He doesn't understand it. He doesn't even understand the questions. He's always preferred to be left alone, but nothing would do that. Not the ghosts. Not the vampires. Not the damned demon. And not the god he'd mistakenly called a vaudoux.

He's made so many mistakes.

He wipes a tear from his eyes. An honest salt-filled tear. Not something obscure, not something broken and twisted and distorted to mean something entirely different. It falls silently and warmly on his cheek.

Change is something he'd never understood. Especially when it's happening to him.

In the dark, between the shadows, three figures creep upwards. They are invisible, or as invisible as anything could be. They are insubstantial, but not ghosts. They don't seem to acknowledge the sleepers, don't even seem to notice them. That isn't Jack's doing. Anastasia had said, *we are two of the most powerful forces to ever exist*.

Just as quickly as night had fallen, morning arrives. Orange light falls like a firestorm through the interior of the stairs. The suddenness of it startles him.

"Morning," Anastasia says, stepping toward the edge of the stairs to look up into the sky. Even she, a creature of the light, shields her eyes from its intensity.

"It's been morning," Alexis says, stretching his arms as he stands. "Light falls differently in a place like this."

"The caravan will reach the top without us," Anastasia says. "I can see the blue of the sky from here."

Alexis steps beside her, glances up, and says, "So can I."

2.

Something moves through the darkness, the shadows, the corners just beyond the peripheral vision of even the mother, even the DarkWalker. It slithers and stalks, it slides, it glides, and it makes no sound because it doesn't touch the ground.

It's emerged from the statue of a god, a fountain, a pool of water. Roughly human in shape, its smile seems almost real, but its eyes are too far apart, mere wisps of smoke in its ethereal body.

It reaches Jack Harlow while the others stare into the sunlight.

It reaches Jack Harlow and envelops him before he even knows it exists.

It slips into his nose and between his lips to clog his throat. It covers his eyes with two, three, four layers of obscurity. It breathes ice on the back of Jack's neck. The only sound it makes is with its teeth.

And it slips into Jack's mind. A quick thought, a quick word, a suggestion or a hint, something Jack Harlow's barely able to understand.

And then it's gone.

Jack whirls on it, to fight something that isn't there. His heart races in a way it hasn't in a long time. "Who's there?"

The shadows and crevices give no response. He doesn't believe there's no response to be had.

"If we move swiftly," Anastasia says, "we can reach the surface before sunset."

The word *surface* seems wrong, but Jack doesn't question it.

They walk at Alexis's pace. The blindness doesn't seem to slow him much, but he's the most human of them and therefore the slowest. This doesn't seem to bother Anastasia. She smiles a lot, especially without the scarves to cover her face. It doesn't bother Jack, either, because he's dealing with something internal.

He used to be different. He can feel the shadow oozing around his insides. It leaves an oily trail. It's insubstantial, not a physical thing at all, a parasite of a sort but also a hitchhiker. It's using him to get somewhere, or to get to something.

He doesn't have to allow it.

Even as he walks, a part of him pushes and prods the darkness inside him. He used to have a lot more of that. It's not gone completely. Can it be? Does he have balance now? No. Of course not. He's unstable. There are still voids within him that can be filled by parasites and hitchhikers and who knows what else. With a breath, he sends an electric shock through his body, something to prickle his furthest extremes, to dive into his physical and emotional depths. The shadow is a reflection of himself, his former self, a part of who he's trying to forget, a part of him that didn't exist until Lisa Sparrow was stolen from him.

In a way, he should thank the darkness.

But that's not his intention.

They take a break when Alexis needs to drink. Rainwater still drips down the interior of the stairs. It's the color of bourbon under the full light of day. The closer they get to the top, the brighter that light, and the more radiantly the walls glow. They've been painted in brilliant colors: reds and oranges and yellows, with swirls of blue and gray and even black.

Eventually, Jack realizes the only thing familiar about the darkness inside him now is, in fact, the darkness. It's a part of him he wants to reject. But only the darkness within him, his natural darkness, can do that. He hesitates to embrace it. Briefly, he makes eye contact with Anastasia—a dangerous thing to do, considering the depth and vibrancy of her beauty—but her smile doesn't tell him to do anything. It simply says she trusts him—implicitly, explicitly—to do the right thing, to make the right choices.

Lisa had looked at him in that way.

He closes his eyes. He embraces the darkness within him, his own and the intruder's. He squeezes the violation, shoves it out of him, forces it to take solid form, albeit temporarily.

He delivers a well-placed kick that throws the shadow off the stairs, into the shaft of sunlight, the empty space, and into a long drop.

Alexis, eyeless, not even looking in that direction, says, "I was beginning to think I should say something."

"It'll be back," Jack says.

"Darkness always is," Anastasia says. "But we'll reach the top before it does, and what chance do you think a shadow like that has under the full light of the sun?"

The sun is setting when they reach the top. Sunset paints the clouds orange and red, like fire, like life. It's a vast vista, not the side of a mountain at all anymore, and fields of grass and wheat and flowers flow in every direction. On the distant western horizon, there's a castle.

The caravan waits at the top of the stairs. The caravanner hugs Alexis tightly, whispers private words directly in his ears, then goes to Jack Harlow and hugs him, as well. Whispers. "I owe you for what you did."

"I didn't do anything."

"You're the only reason my brother lives." Then she pushes away, refusing any further argument or attempts at modesty, and goes to the mother.

They examine each other for a moment, Anastasia smiling, a light that competes with the sun. Without a word, the caravanner reaches into a pocket and withdraws a fistful of scarves. Again whispering, but close enough Jack hears it: "To protect the others."

"Thank you, daughter," Anastasia says. She wraps them expertly, hiding her chin, her cheeks, her nose and lips, allowing only her eyes to shine.

"It's a long trek to the horizon," the caravanner says. "Everyone sleep tonight, everyone, except the watch." She looks at Jack Harlow. "*Everyone.*"

"I'll take the first watch," Jack Harlow says.

"You'll do no such thing," Anastasia says. "If I find you're awake tonight, I will cut your throat. If I have any reason to believe you're wandering on one of your private little side missions, I will abandon you. If you are tempted by anything in the dark, you will do *nothing* without my permission."

"I don't understand."

"We, all of us, accompany you on this trek because every single one of us believes in something."

He doesn't interrupt to ask what they believe in.

"But we are off the map now, beyond the realms we know. None of us has ever climbed this high, has ever seen this sun. We're in another realm, and we have no inkling of the perils ahead."

"Best to do as she says," Anastasia says.

The prisoner's wagon has been restored to full size. Somehow, it's easier to move this way. Inside, the prisoner laughs. Maybe only Jack can hear it. It's short lived.

"You will sleep beside me," the caravanner says. "If something wakes you in the dark, you will let me know, or you will make the rest of this journey without us."

"Understood."

The troupe has already made camp. They're scattered in a tight circle just a few hundred meters from the top of the stairs. Purple bruises stretch across the sky. Because the territory is unfamiliar and unknown, they light no fire. They make little noise. They don't tell stories, sing, or laugh. In minutes, it seems that everyone lays on their bedrolls or curls against the side of the prisoner's wagon and sleeps.

Indeed, they're all closer to that wagon now than ever.

Jack checks on his threads. There are still so many, some that wind around the caravan and no further. The indigo thread that led to the old king vibrates, the note plucked on the other end, by the king in another realm. It's a message: *We're still with you*.

Another thread leads straight to the castle.

"What's there?" Jack asks the caravanner after they've laid down to sleep. He keeps his voice low enough so the wind doesn't carry it.

"We'll find out in a few days."

3.

The night passes without incident, though Jack Harlow hardly sleeps through it. He dreams, briefly, but recalls nothing when he wakes—which he does multiple times during the night. He's nocturnal, or used to be, so sleeping through the night isn't normal. There are the sounds of ravens and crows and magpies, owls and hawks, critters making their way through the grasses, bigger animals moving through the stalks of wheat and corn. The moon is near full, bright and yellow, familiar in size and shape. She gives Jack comfort. But he can't quite see all the things under the moon. He has no idea what waits at that ruin of a castle.

It's not entirely random; some of this land had been farmed, but long ago, so it's gone a bit wild since then. Jack drifts through the fields in his mind, never stirring, never waking the caravanner, never attracting the attention of the watch. He moves through the bodies of the birds, through the rabbits, through the wolves and the wind and the shadows.

It's a dark realm, and there's something moving through the dark.

Jack snaps to a sitting position. "Get up!" he says.

It's meant as a warning, and everyone responds—but it's too late. One of the wolf soldiers attacks the watch from behind. He never had a chance. The wolf rips open his throat before he falls to the ground.

But it's a distraction. Other wolves come from the other side. Jack is on his feet in an instant. Alexis points out hidden wolves. The troupes respond with silver-tipped arrows. Despite the caravanner's claim that they didn't know what was waiting for them, they prepared.

Jack steps away from the camp, toward a trio of wolves not yet visible. There are maybe ten in total.

They're quick. Vicious. Someone else falls. Jack takes a breath, like the wolf of fairy tales, and launches a concussive wave of energy into the field. The wolves are scattered, and some splattered, bits of fur and meat flying in all directions.

One of the wolves crashes into the side of the prisoner's wagon. Tears at it with her claws. Rips at the wood and the magic beneath it. Anastasia's there, almost right next to it. She says, "No." Nothing else. She makes no move, either defensive or offensive, simply speaks directly to the wolf soldier.

The wolf whimpers. Cowers. Turns tail and runs.

The others still alive run with her.

There's one that's wounded. It doesn't get far. The caravanner slices is throat to end its suffering. Then she looks up to Jack, eyes narrowed—eyes being all that's visible under the face scarves—and says, "You called them."

"I did not." He's too shocked to argue. Why would she even think that?

The wolves howl as they flee. But they do flee, further and further away. Jack and Alexis watch for as long as they can.

They lost two in the attack. The troupe is down to nine total, including Jack but excluding the prisoner.

They dig shallow graves, completing the work before dawn, to bury their dead. The dawn is explosive, a thick array of reds dancing across the sky. It's an inappropriate tone for the task at hand. The burial is quick. The caravanner's eulogy is brief. "Amira. Maalick. You will be missed."

Jack realizes he hardly knew them. That's not unusual. He's often traveled with strangers. It seems to be his curse.

"Now, at least, we know what kinds of lands these are," the caravanner says. "Dark lands."

"Twilight lands," Anastasia corrects. "Some lean more heavily toward the dark, but look around. This is no hellscape."

But to the troupe, it feels like a hellscape. They cannot remember the last time they lost two together. They have a makeshift wake under the light of dawn, which lasts a long while, telling stories of others they've lost along the way, stories of Amira and her wicked tongue—tales to make Scheherazade blush—and stories of Maalick's prowess with cards, his preference for jokers, thieves, and assorted faces that never belonged.

Before they cover the bodies, in fact, one of them— Jack doesn't know who—retrieves a pack of cards from Maalick's things. They carry so little, everything must be important. The deck is revealed to be all jokers and jollies and boxers and shadows. "Maalick made each of these cards," someone says, before the deck disappears in someone's pockets as a remembrance.

They fill the graves with dirt. The caravanner whispers a blessing, then says, "Let's move." Anastasia kneels between the graves and spins a little magic, a talisman or a guard of some sort, to protect the bodies from scavengers.

Then they're moving across the vast fields.

The way is slow. The wagon wheels don't like the soft earth. The horses are tentative but unstoppable. The castle never seems to be closer. Indeed, Jack realizes most of the troupe don't see that far into the distance.

"It was a tough night," Al-Qaum says to Jack. They're at the rear of the caravan as they walk. "How are you holding up?"

"I'm fine," Jack says.

"I know you didn't know Maalick or Amira like the others did, but you know that's not what I mean."

"I'm still me, if that's what you mean."

"Still who you are, or still what you are?"

Jack considers that for a moment.

"I really don't think you know who you are," Al-Qaum says. "You have a name, and you sometimes use it, and we try to keep your secret for you, but as important as names may be, they're not what defines us."

The going is slow. The fields stretch forever. The nature of the grass, the dirt, and the things growing shifts. When they stop for meals, they roast fresh corn. Anastasia makes bread from wheat. They catch rabbits. And the castle never seems any closer.

But after several days or a week without incident, without wolves or shadows or fairies trying to tempt Jack into the open, the rest of the troupe at last can see the castle. In the night, the moonlight lessens as she slips through her phases; Jack Harlow sees things under the light of the moon, but cannot see into the castle. It remains a mystery. An enigma. It's protected, or at least shielded, from casual spying, and Jack isn't ready yet to focus more energy on it.

Their path crosses the wolf soldiers by day some days later. The wolves continue on their way, giving only nasty looks. Two are wounded, one limping, all of them skittish of the caravan.

As they travel, Al-Qaum tells the most stories. He takes center stage on the second night to tell about the time Amira got into an argument with an elephant. The elephant won by default. The next night, he tells about when Maalick tried to swim across an oasis pond, but since it was all of half a meter in depth, it was a losing proposition.

After that, he tells of a dancing dervish, a wish-granting djinn with an ulterior motive, a British king who had saved the ravens, and even something from the DarkWalker's past, a story about the Prince of the Stable Door. It's an old story involving chickens and a princess and a military caravan in a wilder age.

The acrobat tells of his days touring with the circus, but it's a sad story, and in the end everyone dies. When Alexis gets up to tell a story, he talks about his new vision. "I see colors I never knew existed. I see shadows and storms. I see blood pumping in your veins, and I see thoughts drifting through your brains. It's hard to get used to, mostly noise now, I can't actually read any of that, but I know it means something. And I can see the castle, all the way to the castle walls. It's a ruin, and I know it's where we're headed. There are people there, but it's not a country anymore. It's been reclaimed. I can't see them." He turns his head toward Jack. "I doubt anyone can, to be honest. But it's a dangerous place filled with dangerous people, and I know they see us, as well."

One morning, a wanderer hails them. He approaches tentatively but openly. As far as Jack can tell, the man's alone. He wants to trade meat for water. "It ain't been rainin'," he says, though they know this.

"We don't need meat," the caravanner says. "Tell us about the castle."

The wanderer looks over his shoulder. "There's not much to tell. No one goes into the castle anymore. It's been overrun."

"Overrun by what?"

"Ghosts."

For some reason, this gives Jack hope. He knows, intuitively, where the ghosts came from.

"Have you been to Shangri La in your travels?" Jack asks.

Everyone looks at him. He hasn't mentioned Shangri La at all.

"No one goes to Shangri La anymore," the wanderer says. "Not since the war brought down the mountain, not since the dead descended on what were supposed to be sacred lands."

"I don't understand."

"Shangri La has been unmade," the wanderer says. "I don't believe that's news. It's an old story by now."

"What of the people there?" Jack asks.

The wanderer shrugs. "Who can say? Nomads, vagabonds, listless and restless, they're probably just wanderers now."

It's a strong hint of something. Jack tilts his head, tries to see better into the wanderer. "Have we met?"

The wanderer shakes his head. "I believe I'd remember."

Jack isn't sure about that. "You were at Shangri La when Armageddon came down?"

He shakes his head again. "No, I arrived after. I was wandering, following my heart, following a light in my soul, but it led me astray." He sighs. "I'm still searching for that part of me I lost there."

"Here, drink," the caravanner says, offering a skin of water. "We've also got wine, if you'd like some."

The wanderer thanks her, but refuses the wine. When he leaves them, he travels toward neither the castle nor the stairs they had come by.

"Is he safe on his own out there?" one the troupe asks.

"He's more than he appears," Anastasia says. "There's no help we can give him. He has his own story to unfold."

Days stretch, weeks stretch, until Jack can see a sign of the baby inside Anastasia's belly. It's only just the beginning of a bulge. She's barely lost any of her pace. No one else would notice. Jack's pace is off, too. As they get closer to the castle—it now seems to get bigger against the horizon, so they're making real and measurable progress—a pit grows in his stomach. This isn't something invading or intruding, it's no parasite, no hitchhiker, it's merely a growing certainty there's something wrong with the castle.

But the thread that connects him to someone or something in that castle, or to the castle itself, becomes brighter and more resonant as they approach. He sees the ravens flying around it now. He hears the sounds of heartbeats.

And he sees, in the distance, the three shadowy figures that have been following him since death.

4.

Jack tries to get closer to the shadows, but he can't. They're slippery. There's no active resistance; it's just that they defy easy observation. It's part of their nature. He almost recognizes them, or their nature, but he isn't sure—and is less sure of their intentions.

They're closer to the castle, maybe only a couple of days away now, and surely they're watching the caravan approach. How could they not?

The moon disappears for a night or two, then reemerges, as moons tend to do. The nights get longer, the days cooler. Beyond the castle, the snowy peaks of mountains come into view. When they climbed the stairs, they hadn't reached the top of a mountain so much as entered another realm.

The number of wolf soldiers patrolling the fields grows. They pass farmsteads, barns and houses, herds of cattle, the sons of farmers who eye them suspiciously. Once or twice, the caravanner stops to greet someone, to trade for milk and eggs, but the caravan's supplies run thin. There's little by way of silk or spice to trade. No one would want the prisoner's wagon. It cannot easily be opened, from the inside or out, and who would willingly bear the responsibility of releasing the prisoner?

When Jack asks about the prisoner, the caravanner only says he's her family's responsibility, he's been hers alone for almost a thousand years. Alexis and Al-Qaum are part of her extended family, but she's got no brothers, no sisters left alive. Her mother, her birth mother, disappeared during the Ravagers' Wars. Her father was a rogue; the less said about him, the better.

Anastasia deflects every conversation. She talks about prisoners of the ages: the man in the iron mask, the ghosts in the Tower, Port Arthur with is criminals and orphans, Persephone.

"You're being evasive," Jack tells her.

She smiles under her scarves. "And you're prying into things that shouldn't concern you."

"Shouldn't," Jack points out, "is not the same as *don't*."

He asks Al-Qaum about it, too, but all he wants is to tell stories. "A sandstorm came one time, twenty seasons ago maybe. I was travelling with the caravan that year, but the sandstorm, that was unexpected. It scattered the caravan. We never did find everyone after. Buried in the sand, picked alive by starved vultures, we could only make guesses. For three days, the prisoner was lost, buried in the sand as the storm intensified. You know, they say the storm was because a princess angered the gods. They say it was a fat, ugly dervish mourning the death of his blind mistress. They say the storm stretched across a half dozen other realms, and that it was reality itself reacting to the fall of Paradise. But in the end, Paradise turned out to be a gambler's den half a day's ride into the wastelands."

Jack shakes his head. "None of that's helpful."

"Well, Paradise is still there, and I'm sure you can convince the bones to roll your way, should you go," Al-Qaum says, "but I'm not the gambling type. As to the sandstorm—you've never seen such a wicked storm. The sands outside Babylon are gray, but others sands are brown, dusty, dusky, and crimson. We were near a borderlands, so we had sand like blood on one side, sand like shadows on the other. There was no shelter to be found. The best we could do was stay low. But the winds were strong. They say the sands blasted skin off the flesh of other caravans, but I don't know that there's any truth there."

He lowers his voice to continue. "But you can ask Asteria, and she'll agree with me on this: our prisoner summoned that sandstorm. It was an escape attempt.

And it failed."

In the night, as everyone sleeps, when Jack takes a turn at watch, he walks the perimeter. He watches the movement of wolf soldiers, farmers' sons, scorpions, and hawks. He pauses at the prisoner's wagon several times. He hears the prisoner's breaths. Shallow things. They can't be shallow, if he can hear them. The prisoner has been quiet. He must be up to something.

Jack knocks twice on the wagon's door. Little, quiet taps. No one in the caravan hears it. "Who are you?" he asks.

One of his threads, one of the weak ones, which changes in color and intensity but tends to hide from him, has always led to the prisoner's cart. That could be because they travel with the same caravan, but there might be something else. It's the only thread that sometimes carries the same indigo that leads back to the king.

And that indigo thread connects from the king to the prisoner, as well.

It's the first time Jack's seen a thread that doesn't connect directly to him, but there is a relationship between the three of them. Briefly, the separate threads wind about each other, pulsate, sing a note too deep for human ears, too soft to interrupt the dreams of sleeping caravanners.

Jack touches the threads. They vibrate together, as if part of the same song. And briefly, there's an electricity to it, enough that it shocks Jack and leaves a bit of ash on his fingers.

"Who are you?" he whispers.

On the opposite side of the door, no further away than the thickness of that wood and the potency of that magic, the prisoner whispers back. "Who are *you*?"

Jack hesitates to reveal his name. The prisoner, however, has been in that wagon for longer than Jack's been alive, and his name's been given voice within the prisoner's earshot before. He says, tentatively, "Jack Harlow."

"Jack Harlow," the prisoner says back.

"Who are you?"

"I'm tired. Let me sleep."

The sound of breathing, even the sound of wind across the fields, goes suddenly quiet. Anastasia sits up from her sleep and looks directly at Jack. She rushes forward with a speed he'd never imagined. She takes him by the collarbone, by the waist, and throws him a hundred meters into the fields. They land on his back. She's on top of him. The scarves around her mouth drip so he can see her lips as well as her eyes.

In a whisper, she says, "Leave it."

Jack takes a breath. "I don't think I can."

She kisses him. Briefly and quickly. Tenderly. Then she lays her head on his chest and cries. It's gentle, and quiet, and until the first drop falls on his chest, he's not even sure that's what's happening. "No one can protect you from the prisoner inside."

"Are you sure I need protection?"

"Are you sure you don't?" She sighs. "You're still weak, love, and you're still learning. The prisoner has ten thousand years on you. Ten thousand years of experience, of strength, of time to think and plan and plot. He knows what he wants, when the time comes for him to be freed."

"When will that time come?"

She shakes her head. "Sooner than I wish."

"What was his crime?" Jack asks.

She touches his lips with her finger, lets it linger for a moment, then pushes herself upright again. "Crimes," she says, correcting him. "Tonight, at the fire, I'll tell the tale."

5.

At noon, high noon or something like it, a delegation from the castle meets the caravan. There are nine—matching the caravan in number if not in strength. They carry no flag or banner. There's no indication of nation, country, or tribe. One among them, presumably not the actual leader but the woman assigned the role of negotiator, dismounts from her horse and says to the caravanner, in a voice loud enough for all to hear: "You will not be welcome in the castle, but you will not be turned away from the doors. You may make camp outside the ramparts, where you will be watched severely, and where bowmen will be constantly at the ready. Only one among you may enter the castle, and only when we send someone to retrieve you."

"Only one?" the caravanner asks. "One in particular?"

"This, I haven't been told."

"Whose castle was it?" Al-Qaum asks.

"It doesn't matter, whose it was," the negotiator says. "It is ours now, and these lands are slowly being brought back to life after a long, frozen winter. The warriors inside have fought frost and ice, giants and walkers and even the dead. We beg that you not add the weight of your souls to our burden."

Then she returns to her horse. The delegation goes back. Their horses move swiftly and surely, and they disappear from sight before they reach the castle walls.

"Nothing changes," the caravanner announces. "Our road leads through that castle. They will, ultimately, let us pass."

It sounds almost like a threat. Perhaps it is. While the negotiator spoke, the others in the delegation studied the members of the caravan. Two had regarded Jack Harlow, and another two had lingered over Anastasia.

Even with only her eyes visible, her beauty emanates from her like from a pulsar. Being in near proximity for so long, Jack forgets the full power of her presence. The delegates, however, took note of every heartbeat, every breath, every movement of her eyes.

"They didn't really have a message," Alexis says, echoing Jack's own thoughts. "They came to determine who we were."

"What have they learned?"

Alexis says, "Everything."

The word echoes into silence. Finally the caravanner says, "We have nothing to hide. We go forward."

They stop for the night not far from the castle. It's less than a day's walk now. Sentries on the ramparts are visible. Wagons and horses and people pass in and out of the gates. Clouds streak across the sky, swirling, moving faster but still not promising rain.

At sunfall, they lock the gates.

The caravan makes a bonfire. There's no point in trying to hide, and they're close enough now to the castle that there seems less risk of predators. They don't remember the last time they saw wolf soldiers up close.

Jack, however, sees the sentries are, in fact, wolf soldiers.

The days are short, nearly half the length of the night, so they're not thoroughly exhausted. They settle for the night, pass around bottles of wine, roast meat over the fire, and tell stories.

Al-Qaum tells of a prince who set out in search of his princess only to fall in love with a witch. Alexis's story follows a sailor in the clouds hunting stray lightning bolts for one of the old gods. Another story highlights the magic of music, and another touches on the virtues and vices of snow.

"I would tell a story," Anastasia says.

This is rare. Everyone goes immediately quiet. The caravanner, noticeably, is apprehensive. She leans forward where she sits, and repeatedly darts looks at Jack Harlow as though he's done something incredibly wrong.

6.

Once upon a time, in a land far from here, where those still living ran around without any clue of what awaited and the things around them, there was born a man of enormous hatred. It was inherent in him, there from the start, as though something in his make-up had been wrong and rotten before birth. However, it would be wrong to blame his mother, as she was a woman of great kindness and warmth. But she was also a power—known to bring rain for the growing and sunshine for the harvest. She held back plagues, and during a drought created the bottomless lake from a single tear.

Her child, her son, displayed none of these abilities, not at first. Instead, he was seen to coax a flower from blooming to wilting. He ate insects. He hurt other children and had to be kept in a tower.

He was given everything. Books. Music. Poetry. The finest chefs came from all corners of the earth to prepare his meals. When he was a teenager, he transmuted noodles into worms, which he then consumed alive. When he got older, he drew women to his tower and convinced them to climb to his window.

He called other things to the tower, too. Fire. Locusts. Armies from hell led by the Prince of Thorns himself. It was a horrible time, and his mother—she did what she could to appease him.

Eventually, he seduced a princess. She sacrificed herself to break the walls of his tower, though he needed only to climb out the window. Nothing held him there. Nothing bound him. She took hemlock, and stabbed herself with the gold and onyx dagger whose name even I don't dare speak. Thus bleeding, she threw herself from the window of his tower. When she hit the earth, it rumbled, the tower cracked and fell, the seas rose, and the whole of the country was swallowed by the ocean.

He floated across the ocean for a good many years, wrestling winds and squid, traveling within the bellies of whales, sometimes hitching a ride under the hulls of sailboats. He sailed with conquerors, Vikings and the like, and often laid waste to whole villages and entire islands, taking prisoners of his own to keep for days, weeks, or years, depending on his proclivities at the time.

He was a nasty man. He could kill with a look, with a thought, and even by inadvertence. A thousand and one of the strongest, most powerful, most terrifying creatures of the night and of the day tried to take him down during an eclipse, but even combined they were no match for him. He knew it and they knew it.

In the course of their conflict, he cracked the earth.

He buried a thousand and one of the greatest heroes of an age in fault lines he'd created, then also a thousand and one villages, towns, and cities. The good and the bad. The innocent and the guilty. It took a century for the fires to be doused. Longer for some mountains to rise again. Some empires simply didn't.

You might ask, if his mother was such a good and benevolent force, how had he come to be so bad? Was it the fault of his father? It wasn't. Not at all, not in any way. Had there been a corrupting influence from elsewhere? No. His evil, his lack of compassion, his blatant disregard for the fate of the planet, was in him from the start because it was in his mother.

You might think she was a creature of the light from the moment of her birth, but there are few today who know the truth of her. Even the prisoner has no idea what his mother was capable of, what she had done. In the end, she had made a choice: to stand on the side of light, to do good things, to commune with the gods of sunlight and mercy.

He never made that choice.

He hasn't made that choice yet.

When his mother came to put him down, to punish him, to make him atone for his crimes, he ridiculed her, and he annihilated her. Smote her from existence. It was an awful day. The effort cost both their lives. Mother and son. They died, and thus the earth was spared whatever might have happened after.

In other realms, they were of course both remade, reborn, and revived. And there, with the help of another entity of great power, she constructed a prison to hold her son, and she entrusted the caring of that prison to— well, to one of her adoptive daughters at the gates of Babylon.

You know that story.

7.

The caravan goes utterly silent when Anastasia finishes her story. She steps away from the fire, away from the camp, to the far side of the prisoner's wagon. She sighs heavily and looks up to the moon. The half moon mocks her.

Most of the caravan breaks away from the bonfire. It's time to sleep, or to lay in silent contemplation of things unknowable. After leaving her alone for a short while, Jack walks past the prisoner's wagon—he's crying inside there, Jack's sure of it—and stands beside the mother of the story.

He doesn't say anything. What could words do? He puts an arm around her shoulders and lets her rest her head on his. The stars look down seemingly without interest. The moon glimmers. Jack's shadows are far, far away, hiding along the horizon. Perhaps they heard the story. Perhaps every farmer's son, wolf, and castle sentry heard the story.

"It's a story I've never told," she says. "Now you know his crimes, but not mine."

Jack shakes his head. "I don't need to know your crimes."

"Don't you?"

"The past doesn't change who you are."

"The past defines who we were."

Jack shakes his head. "Those are not the same people."

They stand together a while longer, under the moon and the stars, near the end of a great expanse of fields and meadows and woodland, half a day's walk from a castle that promises secrets. One of the threads connects Jack to someone inside that castle, or to the castle itself. He's not nervous, not scared, but more than a little curious. In the past, he's never really acted upon his curiosities before. He would have argued that he'd had none, he merely wished to be left alone.

Even death, at the hands of the DarkCrawler, didn't bring him someplace where he could be left alone.

"You'll have to go into the castle by yourself," Anastasia says.

"I don't think we'll be given a choice."

"You misunderstand. You are not part of this caravan." Again, she leaves out his name, but he sees it on the tip of her tongue. She turns to him, touches his cheek. "We'll arrive by noon, and face whatever we might face. You must go before us. Tonight."

He doesn't argue. He doesn't resist. They stand a while longer, maybe taking comfort in the nearness of their opposing strengths, the dark and the light together in this twilight realm. When he goes, not a single person in the caravan doesn't watch him. Even Alexis, without eyes, knows Jack's leaving the caravan, and perhaps sees more than Jack can see. The caravanner, sitting still near the fire, pointedly puts her back to him. And Al-Qaum, far from the fire, smiles and whispers—though the words shouldn't reach Jack across that distance—"We'll meet again, and stand with you when the time comes."

Jack doesn't know what time might come. He takes a breath and travels forward. Even the eyes of the prisoner, through the magic and the wagon, are heavy on his back. In the past, Jack has faced dangers alone and with friends, allies, or—it's a word he might not have used before—supplicants.

Jack walks quickly toward the castle, unencumbered by the caravan around him, the horses, the people, the stories they tell. He has a story to live inside the castle, and, should he survive it, beyond the castle.

He knows where he's going in the end. To find Lisa Sparrow. To rescue her. He's going to a place he probably should have gone from the start. He's never been smart enough to take action, only to react—but in at least one case, he failed to react properly.

There was a start to everything, a beginning, and it wasn't the night of his birthday when the ghost kissed him in that basement; it wasn't the night his sister and father betrayed him; it wasn't even the death of his own mother. It wasn't the trickster godling who let Jack believe he was merely a vaudoux. It wasn't even Lisa Sparrow, whose love—whose very presence—might have changed his life.

There's something more. Something worse. Something darker than all of that at the end of this road. But first, before any of that, he must confront the castle.

The moon hangs low in the west when he reaches the castle gates. Sentries and guards look down at him, but most don't say a word or even move. They know who he is, what he is. They sent a delegation to confirm if it was true. It was.

Jack Harlow is the DarkWalker, the Destroyer of Hells, and he's walked across a vast expanse of other realms to come to their gates.

They don't even bother trying to resist. Reluctantly, without enthusiasm, the gates are opened. There's a mechanism, a system of pulleys and ropes, and a man physically turning a pegged wooden wheel. The eyes of the caravan behind him, the eyes of the sentries above, even the eyes of the moon watch as he breaches the castle walls. No hand stands against him, but a person— a delegation of one, the negotiator who had met them in the fields—walks to meet him. She smiles, but it's all business and without emotion. She says, "Jack Harlow."

"You know me."

"And the stories of you," the negotiator says. "We were never going to refuse you entry."

"I may not be who I was," Jack tells her.

"You may not be. But—you're still the son of Amelia Harlow."

CHAPTER FIVE

1.

The castle is a ruin. It's overgrown with greenery, bushes and trees and vines that snake through every open space, worsening every crack in the walls, shattering every window. The courtyard beyond the ramparts is a mess of thicket and bramble. It's like walking into the start of a fairy tale where the witch's worst curse had long ago been enacted.

The negotiator stands before Jack Harlow unafraid. She's done nothing, and is planning nothing, so she has no reason for fear. That just means she hasn't heard all the stories. Jack's reputation does not leave a lot of room for mercy. She's tall and thin, her eyes heavily laden, dark around the edges, sallow. He hadn't noticed until he was close to her, or maybe he hadn't been looking.

"What happened here?" Jack asks.

"Nothing happened *here*," she tells him. "We've been waiting for you."

"Why?"

"Every one of us here was in Shangri La when you—cut us loose."

She might have said that any number of ways. "Is that what you think happened?"

"We've been waiting," she says again, "because your mother has been waiting, but she doesn't know if she's safe. So you see me first."

"If you decide I'm not safe?"

"Then I don't tell you where she is."

"Perhaps I could simply pull that information from your head," Jack says. "Or torture you until you give it to me, or slay you and torture the ghost of you. I *am* the DarkWalker, remember."

"You know what happened on the road to Shangri La," she says. "The DarkCrawler came among us and peeled back our souls, scratched and scraped the deepest surfaces of us, poisoned ourselves against ourselves. You think there's anything you can do to rival that?"

She's telling a truth. Jack hadn't being paying attention. He'd had no true idea the extent of the damage the DarkCrawler had caused—and why, because Jack *existed*? He always found it difficult to understand the motivations of madmen.

"Also," the negotiator adds, "we have taken precautions."

Whatever those *precautions* are, Jack doesn't see them.

What he also doesn't see: a large number of people. Sure, it's early, near dawn, and many might be asleep, but now that he's in the castle, he can sense the sparseness of everything. There's almost no one here.

The farmers, the trade, the gates—all of it was a ruse?

"What do I need to do?" Jack asks.

The negotiator smiles. She's had a small triumph, but she's enjoying it. She knows things might have gone differently. A different version of Jack might peel her apart layer by layer, atom by atom, until he gets what he wants.

"There's no test," she says. "No challenge. Just walk with me."

She turns to lead him into the actual castle, but he doesn't move. "What about my friends?"

"Friends?"

"The caravan."

"No one will be here when they arrive," the negotiator says, "so there'll be no one to stop them." She says this with her back to him.

"Where will they go?"

"They'll rediscover their own paths. Slowly, that's what we've all been doing."

"What about you?"

She turns at the waist, at the neck, only to look at him a moment. "I don't believe you really care."

"Maybe I'm only curious," Jack admits. "I don't know what the DarkCrawler did to you, I only know he did it because he wanted me, and you were—nothing more than a battery for him, a source of power. I don't even know why he thought he needed to destroy me."

"Did he succeed?"

He tilts his head. Flexes the fingers at the ends of his hands. "I believe he might have, but he didn't know the meaning of it."

She smiles. "Perhaps you should ask him."

"Do you know what happened after I died?" Jack asks.

"The Angel of Death took him."

Jack takes a breath. He'd met the Angel of Death, spoke with her in the Shallow City. She'd had him sentence her for her crimes, but he'd sentenced her only to time served. He hadn't truly known her crimes—if any—or what time she had served. The Shallow City under Silver Blade might have been a kind of prison for some, but not for her.

"You don't seem all that surprised," the negotiator says.

Jack doesn't have a response. He walks with the negotiator. Leaving the courtyard, they immediately enter a kind of throne room, a reception area, where perhaps the king would entertain guests or see to his people. There are tables, rows of seating, massive chandeliers stripped of their candles. Dried bloodstains indicate where the king had breathed his last. Jack can get a sense of those last moments, the jester's betrayal, the degree of power these walls had witnessed.

The green has overtaken the room. Vines twist around the throne, the tables and chairs, and climb the walls to where a huge hole gapes in the ceiling. There's no rubble visible. All light that comes into the throne room is courtesy of the first hints of dawn.

"Why will everyone leave?" Jack asks. "I thought this realm was being reclaimed."

"By farmers, first," the negotiator says, "and now by soldiers of the wolf. The farmers don't know any other way. Neither, really, do the wolves."

"They're only wolves," Jack says.

"They're only farmers. And we, here, are only ghosts—echoes and memories of who and what we once were."

"What if there wasn't a wolf?" Jack asks.

"It's hard to speak about hypotheticals. So many of us have left already. We few who remain—we knew why."

"Me?"

"You have quite an ego, don't you?"

"It's been reinforced from the outside," Jack says.

She doesn't answer this. Behind the throne, there's a wide open area leading to double doors—permanently ajar, broken, hanging on hinges and locked by time into place. One is half collapsed under the gravity of excessive ivy and wisteria.

The hall leads to another, then to grand rooms, with windows overlooking a landscape not visible from the outside of the castle: a shoreline, waves crashing against rocks, shattered piers, the glow of dawn making the whole scene appear to be a slow motion explosion.

"We can only guess at the history of this place," the negotiator says, pointing out the skeleton pinned to the bed by a rotted crossbow shaft, others pinned to the walls. "We don't sleep where they left the bodies to rot. We're not convinced they're any more dead than we are."

"Who were you before?" Jack asks. It's the question he never got to ask Claire Winters, the ghost who had sacrificed herself for Jack not once but twice. He doesn't want to make that mistake again.

"I was alive."

It's not the answer he wants, but for the moment it's all she seems willing to give.

The next series of rooms have no ceiling at all. A forest dominates them, the trunks of the trees as thick as Jack himself. They're tall, and must have had decades, at least, to grow like that. But he knows time is weird in the other realms. He remembers his months in a variety of hells had only been minutes on earth.

Birds move from branch to branch. They sing to the rising sun. It's lighter here because the sun is higher, the roiling clouds still red with the dawn, the relentless sound of the ocean growing.

A wide stairwell descends to a lower level. The castle crumbles in places. Holes let in the light of day, the singing of the ocean. On this lower level, the rubble remains. Walls have been shattered—interior and exterior walls in all directions. The floors are made of stone, but in places there are cracks, there's weakness, there's even unsteadiness. The negotiator steps around these as best she can. Jack follows every step precisely.

"We found a lot of things, when we got here. We found the farmers. That gave them hope, I think. Reason to work the fields again. We found the wolves, and we learned even ghosts can die. We saw you die, and we saw your ghost eradicated, so for a long time we didn't expect you to really arrive here. Your mother, though, knew you were coming. She knew there was no choice."

When she was alive, Jack's mother had been wonderful, a light in his life, the glue that held their family together. In death, he never saw her until the DarkCrawler crept into her fresh bones and veins to distract him. Because of him. No one died in Shangri La except as a means to get at Jack Harlow.

They descend another level. Here, no more windows open onto the ocean, though there are still breaks in the walls. The air is thicker, darker, saturated with odors best left unexplored. "Where are we going?"

"We're almost there," she says.

The threads, those that don't dangle in tatters, hum slightly as they go down yet another set of stairs. The stones are darker here, and damper. Cobwebs hang in the corners, thick strands of them, but the spiders watch from small cracks in the junctures between wall and ceiling. The halls are narrower, and the rooms to either side smaller. Business was done down here, and not the kind of business you preferred to have exposed to sunlight.

In some rooms, the skeletal remains of prisoners are still bound in irons.

Finally, they come to a larger chamber, a kind of theater, with several rows of seating and a raised stage. Two people stand on the stage, but thick shadows drift through the room so they're not readily visible. One is a woman. She steps forward, to the edge of a hole in the stage floor. Something had crashed through there many, many years ago, and the hole now resembles a black pit with sharp wooden teeth.

The woman is his mother. Amelia Harlow. She smiles, and with one hand reaches for him, beckoning, yearning.

He almost doesn't see the thin black necklace she wears, or the matching chain that binds her by the ankle. He almost rushes forward, but he remembers the last thing she ever said to him—as a ghost under the influence of the DarkCrawler—bound by iron, embracing her daughter—*Believe nothing he says*.

He being the DarkCrawler.

The man behind her in the shadows.

He smiles crookedly. Pleased with himself. He says,

"Even the Angel of Death could not prevent us from coming together again. We are—how would you say it—united?" He holds, in one hand, the thread that links them—a thread that is also the chain that binds Jack's mother to him—a thread that is iron and ethereal simultaneously, black like rot.

Jack moves, but the negotiator puts an arm out to stop him. She says in a whisper, "He's stronger than you now."

"He was never stronger than me."

The DarkCrawler draws Jack's mother closer to him, pulling her by the iron thread, which seems to affect the chain around her neck as much as the one at her ankle. Where the iron touches her, the skin molders. Given enough time, that iron will rot through flesh and veins and bone.

When she speaks, Amelia Harlow does so subsonicly. Maybe the DarkCrawler hears it, maybe not. "Don't worry about me, Jack. Run."

But Jack Harlow will do no such thing. Anyhow, he'd never be given the chance. The negotiator's hand on his chest has sprouted tendrils of leafy ivy which even now creep around his body. Behind him, the doorway they'd passed through has thickened with oak limbs and poison-tipped thorns. The only way out, now, is through the DarkCrawler.

Everything about the DarkCrawler is oily, slick, distasteful, disgusting. Jack hadn't noticed before how thoroughly the rot had crawled through the man, the former watcher.

"And now," the DarkCrawler says, "I know I can't end you, just as you can't end me, so I have made other arrangements." He wraps a thread around his wrist, the thin, slimy thread that connects him to the DarkWalker, and pulls.

Jack cuts it.

He cuts the thread with a fingernail as sharp as any assassin's blade. The thread bleeds rot and decay. Jack steps away from it, dragging the negotiator and her brambles with him. She's only half human now, half flora, but even the root system of a thousand year old cypress couldn't resist Jack's sudden surge of strength. It comes from deep within him. Maybe those distant cypresses lend him the power. It's not the strength of the DarkWalker he calls on to step away and break free.

And though it hurts the negotiator, though she screams in pain as he tears through her viny limbs, though she drops to her knees and bleeds red and green bloods together, he leaps forward. Though the DarkCrawler had tried to pull him, Jack breaks the rhythm. The DarkCrawler only stumbles back a single step before righting himself.

In that same instant, Jack is there, striking his chest with every ounce of power ever imagined. The weight of suns, the gravity of the moon, the force of a thousand nuclear bombs. The iron threads that hold Jack's mother shatter. Splinters pierce his back.

The power is more than the DarkCrawler can withstand. But he manages to say, "Oops."

Behind Jack, the wood floor cracks in seemingly random places. Shards drop into the black hole. It has its own gravity. And it has Amelia Harlow. Her footing is gone. Though she flails, there's nothing to catch hold of, so she falls.

There's no bottom to the hole. There are no easily definable dimensions of any sort. It falls in on itself, folds over and around itself, snakes through an endless maze of nothingness.

When Jack turns to look, too late to catch his mother before she falls, the DarkCrawler responds with an attack of his own. A mere push, it's stronger than the cypresses, and robs Jack of his balance. He tumbles in after his mother.

But he's the DarkWalker. Or *something*. He's a strength and power of his own. He catches hold of the very air, defies gravity, refuses to plunge into a prison made exclusively for him. With one free hand, he catches the thread that connects him and his mother. It takes physical form, albeit briefly. He pulls her out of the gaping mouth to nowhere. And he catches a thread still connecting him to the DarkCrawler—a new connection has already been made—and drags him forward.

The DarkCrawler falls into the pit.

Jack severs the final thread that connects them.

He lands on stage, on the far side of the hole, clutching his mother in one arm. He brings down the ceiling on top of the hole, sending spears and shards after the DarkCrawler, though there's no need. But it's no final act of cruelty. It's not to skewer the DarkCrawler as he falls. It's to bury the hole and seal the dimension.

It requires more than mere wood and stone. It requires concentration, an enormous amount of energy and willpower, and almost every breath he's got left. When he's done, when the black pit has been buried beyond the reach of man or ghost, so that the prison dimension folds infinitely on itself with no hope for escape to anyplace else, Jack Harlow slumps in his mother's arms. She holds him. The negotiator cries from the stairs. The little theater plunges into darkness. No, it's Jack who's plunged into darkness. He passes out.

His mother guides his fall, protects his head, cradles him like a mother would. She says his name—not his full name, just *Jack*—over and over again. She caresses his cheek. "My son," she says, intermittently.

His eyes flutter. Hs reaches up to hold her hand. He says, "He's gone."

"And it almost took everything out of you."

Jack smiles. He takes a breath or two. Allows feeling to return to his extremities. "There was never a chance of that." It's a boast, but it's the kind of boast any child would make to his mom.

2.

When the caravan passes through the gates, there's no one in the courtyard and no one in the castle.

"Find safe shelter," the caravanner says. "I want to know what happened to everyone. There were people here even as we approached the gates."

"They've fled," their mother says, kneeling and touching the earth. "They felt the reverberations of our approach, and fear drove them on to other realms."

"How? This isn't a borderlands." The caravanner narrows her eyes, scanning the ruins. "Is it?"

"Sometimes, you don't need borders to cross them. Do you hear that?"

The caravanner says nothing. She listens. She hears the wind and the birds, the work of farmers in distant fields, but not much else—until the sound is inescapable. "Is that an ocean?" But there's mountains beyond the castle, not oceans. Fields stretch in every direction to forests. Wolves howl, even under the noonday sun. The realm trembles, but only briefly, and things have shifted in ways the caravanner can never know. She meets her mother's eyes and says, "Where are we?"

"I believe our path," her mother says, "will require a boat."

The caravanner calls her brothers to her. Alexis. Al-Qaum. "We'll camp here tonight, but first thing in the morning, I want to move on. I don't know if we'll catch up to him, but we have to try. Go, find a road to that ocean, find us a ship, make sure we have a means to move on."

Her brothers leave, not soldiers with orders so much as co-conspirators.

Her mother, Anastasia, has moved to stand within the open gates. She looks back the way they came and smiles softly.

"What do you see?" the caravanner asks.

Anastasia shakes her head one time. "There's a storm ahead."

3.

The negotiator is broken. Part of her was transformed, against her will, into greenery, some of which was torn apart by Jack when he broke free of her grasp. She passes out between sessions of hyperventilation. The pain is more than she can endure. Some of her veins have shifted to ivy. Blood and sap flow through them. The sap coagulates in places. Her left arm had been replaced by twigs and vines and thin branches; the fingers on her right blacken from the lack of oxygen. An amalgamation of her former self and the flora that threatens to take down the whole castle, the transformations were never meant to be long-lasting or self-sufficient.

Traces of the DarkCrawler's rot flow through her, too, caught by blood cells, trapped in places, burning through her insides like a kind of acid. There's nothing of him left, just the scars of his poisons.

She cries, cries out, writhes in agony. Jack does what he can to ease some of her pain, which mostly involves numbing her flesh and searing nerve endings so they can't transmit pain.

One of her eyelids is a leaf, permanently shut but incompletely, so that a bit of her iris peeks out. When she looks at Jack, she's horrified by the things she can't see through. Fear emanates from her in physical waves. She cannot stand anymore. The muscles of her one complete leg are insufficient; the other leg is partly flesh, partly bark, and immobile.

She can't speak. She wants to, but her throat is overgrown, and her lungs work at a fraction of their former capacity. She makes sounds, but they're far short of words, and nothing like her regular voice.

Jack does the only thing he feels he can. He holds a hand over her nose and mouth, shushes her with gentle, reassuring sounds, and quietly smothers her. She doesn't resist. Eventually, her eyes flutter, her body surrenders, the heart stops pumping, and a part of her dies.

There's another part of her now, in the dark: all plant. There's no sunlight here, only a little water in the air, nothing to sustain her. The death of her plant self will be slower. He doesn't know how much consciousness she retains, but he senses the sparks of synapses in her brain. She's still in there somehow.

At full power, Jack Harlow, DarkWalker, Destroyer of Hells, could have maybe repaired all the damage rather than euthanize her. He might have stopped the life in her with a thought, all the life, so that no part of her continued to suffer. He might have liquefied her body and destroyed every semblance of her mind. Smothering her had seemed a kind of mercy. Now, he's not so sure.

He reaches into her body, through the rotting and mutated flesh, pushing under or over bones until he finds her heart, and crushes it in his fist. Then, tendrils grow from his fingers, little bits of himself, burrowing into her arteries so they can reach out to all points of her body. He finds the plant parts and burns the twisted tissue that combines those to her flesh, and in that way disassembles the two halves of her. It's a long, slow process. His mother watches without a word.

Physically, the two halves of the negotiator come apart. He dissolves the flesh, ends whatever thoughts may have persisted, releases her spirit. He sees only the fact of it. She doesn't linger. She doesn't stay. He makes no attempt to find out where she goes.

He pulls his hand free. It looks like a normal hand. He caresses the twigs, the leaves, the vines of the negotiator, searching for any indication of suffering. And it's there, because she needs sunlight to breathe and survive. She's smothering, still, in plant form.

One of the walls of the theater opens onto that ocean. Jack looks from one wall to another, but it doesn't require a lot of effort to sense so great a body of water on the other side of a rock wall, no matter how thick.

The water belongs to another realm, or will carry him—them—to one.

Used to be, he could just blast a hole in the wall with his mind. He had been absurdly powerful. Now, he goes and does the physical work. He taps on a single rock with the butt of his fist until he loosens it, then with a series of blows, pulverizes it, pounds it into dust and memory. Ocean air bursts through that hole. Those winds help him pull away other parts of the wall, widening that hole, until it's massive, until it's big enough for a person, for people, for a wagon carrying a prisoner to break through.

It's not until he's done that he realizes he's bloodied his hands in the process, that he's worked up a sweat. Not long ago, he did manual labor as a means of survival. This was the biggest such job he's ever done.

Sunlight doesn't enter through that hole, though. It's nighttime. A full moon hangs over the ocean. Otherwise, it's a dark sea, infinite and impenetrable.

The process of putting the negotiator beyond the reach of misery takes hours. In a way, she's now a living memorial to all the victims of the DarkCrawler. Amelia Harlow, mother of the DarkWalker, sits on the edge of the stage and watches silently. Now that it's over, now that Jack stands at the edge of the hole he'd made in the side of the castle, she stands and says, "I'm sorry."

"Sorry for what?"

"For everything," she says. "For leaving you the way I did."

"You were killed in the field," Jack says.

"I didn't have to be there."

He shakes his head. "You can't apologize for things that happened to you." He doesn't turn to look at her, though he's acutely aware of how far away from him she is. He can't read his mom, not in the way he can read so many others; he knows she's afraid, but not what of. Afraid of him? Or afraid of her own perceived mistakes? "You were a wonderful mom."

She sighs with that, a release of personal tension. "I'm glad you think so. Because I don't." She takes a breath and adds, "There's other things to apologize for."

"The lies," Jack says.

When she doesn't say anything, he adds, "That's the only thing I want to know about. The lies."

"I wasn't strong enough not to."

He shakes his head.

"Your father had more to say about that than I."

"My *father*?"

She sits again. He doesn't hear it so much as sense the shifting of air behind him. "Whatever he told you," she says, "he was, and always will be, your father."

On the ocean, among the waves, which are strong, and capped with white at the shore, there's a ship, a single light swaying in what appears to be the lead-up to a storm. An unnatural storm. Or preternatural. Jack's not sure he can discern the difference.

"What did he tell you?"

Jack shakes his head. "Doesn't matter. Everything he ever said was a lie."

"That can't be true."

"Feels that way," Jack says. "That makes it true."

In the distance, there's lightning, impossibly long arcs hopping from cloud to cloud to cloud, flashing soundlessly against the sky. It's too distant now, but eventually that storm will overtake the ship and destroy it. The moon, visible only moments before, is now completely obscured.

That doesn't stop Jack from looking. He gives his mom time to say something else.

The crew of the ship scrambles. There's water on the decks, water and blood. They're barely alive, some of them, and presumably many more are not. Storm sails are out, two men struggling to keep the wheel and steer successfully away from the storm.

"He was your father," Amelia Harlow says, "but he wasn't alone in that."

Jack turns away from the sailing vessel. He can't help them from this distance. "I don't know what that means."

She averts her gaze. "I didn't really want to tell you. It's not a proper conversation for a mother and her son."

"Tell me anyhow."

"He was—that night, at least, and maybe other nights as well—he was, you could say, a man possessed."

"Possessed?"

"By a spirit." She shakes her head. "No, I should be more precise. By a ghost."

"Any particular ghost?"

She doesn't answer.

"Everything I am," Jack says, "is because of this, isn't it?"

"It was the ghost of a god," she says. And once it's out, she lets it all out. "I couldn't say which god, or goddess, except to say it was an old one, very old, from before the time of Olympus, before Anubis, before the Sumerians, maybe before the gods of ice and fire. They came into Jonathan—willingly, I might add, your father was always an explorer, an adventurer, a risk-taker—and I was willing, too. We didn't know what would happen, or what could happen, or that anything would happen at all. We were young, foolhardy, and at the time, we believed in our immunities."

Jack looks at her. Every word, every emotion, every unspoken gesture, rings true. Part of him wants to cry. Part of him wants to scream. Part of him only wants to hold onto his mother and never let her go.

He opens his arms. She rushes to him, envelops him in a motherly embrace, her tears wetting his shoulder. "Oh, how I've missed you, Jack."

"And I've missed you."

After a minute of this, she pulls away, not more than arm's length, and looks her son in the eye. "So tell me. What have you done with my Mustang?"

4.

Al-Qaum and Alexis descend through various levels of the castle. The greenery is everywhere. Leaves and ivy and moss, it's as though nature had defeated an army here and staked a claim.

Several times, Alexis stops to look at something—without eyes, through a blindfold—something Al-Qaum cannot see—but he always says, "It's nothing."

"I've never seen so thick a forest," Al-Qaum says. He's spent most of his life in Babylon and the deserts surrounding it, but in his youth, he had been quite an adventurer. He's seen forests and woodlands, though usually in mountains rather than castles, and he's seen lakes reputed to be bottomless. He would readily admit to a fear of such depths, partly because he doesn't know how to swim and partly because he saw what rose from that lake during a fiery sunset.

They've already descended several levels of stairs on the outside of a castle wall facing an impossible ocean. The forest has broken through the stone walls, and the ivy stretches like a spider's web across the large smooth wall beside them. As they descend, the green gives way to yellows—yellow fronds, yellow vines, yellow catching the light of the distant moon behind them. Ahead, on the ocean, there's no sky visible above the storm clouds. The lightning and thunder move closer, and will soon overtake the pier and the castle.

There's no ship moored in the nearby waters, not that he can see, but there's something rising and falling on the dark horizon: a ship racing the storm. They're going to lose, but they're coming this way.

"You see that?" Al-Qaum asks.

"Is that supposed to be a joke?"

"Is it, brother?"

Alexis smiles. "Actually, yes. And yes, I do see it. A ship. All hands—all remaining hands—on deck. They're not alone."

"What do you mean, they're not alone?"

"We should go back," Alexis says. "Tell mother this isn't the way to go."

"What way would you have us go, then?"

Alexis doesn't have an answer for that.

"Wait here," Al-Qaum says, "and watch them carefully. They're coming to this pier." It's still several levels below, but clearly these are the right stairs to take them there. "That storm will catch up to them first. I don't want to see them go under."

"Be quick," Alexis says. "And warn her. There may be danger here beyond our capacity."

Al-Qaum retreats up the stairs, taking them two at a time, racing against the same storm as the ship. He hears no thunder, but the lightning is growing frantic at his back, flashing repeatedly, frequent enough to almost think it's a code of some sort.

These aren't the stairs they'd climbed some weeks or months back—time gets tricky in other realms—but the muscles in his legs scream at the strain. They're much more accustomed to the sands of Babylon. He's not as young as he used to be. He misses his home, the food, the women, the music, the stories. After this journey, perhaps, he'll never venture out of Babylon again.

At the top of the stairs, with the storm at his back and clear sky ahead, in the light of a nearly full moon, he sees a figure—he assumes at first it's someone from the caravan—cutting through the shadows. It's gotten dark, and the dark has thickened, and he feels suddenly that something's wrong.

He draws his knives.

It's not enough to help him. The thing darts in quick, its fur the color of murk, its eyes flashing like brief crystals, and its tail razor edged. It pierces his chest before he even knows it exists. He cries out, once, quickly, and slashes with his blades, but it's too late.

Al-Qaum falls to his side. Life spills out of him. The creature darts back into the shadows, but it bleeds. At least Al-Qaum did not simply surrender to death. He smiles at the notion. He's not sure this counts as honorable, but it's certainly not dishonorable. Despite all probabilities, he died on a quest, on a mythic venture, in service to gods. He'll be remembered in stories.

Al-Qaum closes his eyes and sinks into darkness.

5.

The caravan has circled around itself in the courtyard between ramparts and castle walls to camp for the night. Most of them sleep. The caravanner has climbed a wall, using the vines to pull herself up, so she can see far in multiple directions. She sees the fields behind them, outside the ramparts, where farmers rest from a long day's work, wolves howl, and the moon glides gently across the sky.

The castle is at a border between realms. In another direction, unseen but felt, there's an ocean, an oncoming storm, gale winds, and—something else catches her eye. Something moving, skittering, sneaking around the castle walls. And something not moving, someone not moving, someone she recognizes even collapsed on the ground.

She hops down. The acrobat, keeping watch, knows better than to simply run after her. She races into the dark, drawing a knife from her belt, making as little sound as a summer breeze.

Al-Qaum bleeds.

He sees her, and he smiles, but he hasn't got the strength to lift his head. "I've been skewered," he says. "My story is over."

"No."

There's no sign of the thing that stabbed him. No, there is a sign, there's a drop of its blood, and another drop further off. Al-Qaum's knife is on the ground. He didn't kill it, hardly wounded it from what little there is, but he had drawn blood.

She kneels at his side. "How many?" she asks.

"Just one, I believe. It came out of the dark."

She nods. "Anastasia," she says, not needing to raise her voice.

Their mother is there almost immediately.

She kneels on the other side of him. "You've been stabbed," she says.

"The world goes dark," Al-Qaum tells her.

She smiles, touches his face, leans close, and whispers: "You will not die here, tonight, by this wound. I won't let it happen."

He smiles again. Closes his eyes. Drifts away.

"It's not a fatal wound," Anastasia tells the caravanner. She tears part of his clothes away to reveal where his chest had been pierced.

"It wasn't a big weapon, either."

"No. It was a tail. And it was poisoned. Al-Qaum won't die, and we'll do what we can to make sure of it, but I wouldn't want to dream his dreams right now."

The caravanner nods. "Then I can hunt the thing that did this to him."

"If you must."

"It seems appropriate."

6.

Al-Qaum dreams impossible dreams. He doesn't know it, not immediately, but nothing is real anymore, though he's still in another realm, a kind of dream realm, where dimensions are meaningless, up and down are the same, everything and everyone floats, and all the colors are especially thick and noisy.

He drifts through clouds of cotton candy, led by the scents of cinnamon and jasmine and copper. It's a strange combination, but he doesn't allow it to get to him. He turns over, to look at other colors, other faces, creatures looking down on him with eyes larger than suns. Do they care? They're misshapen, all rough angles and sharp colors. When they speak, their voices reverberate like thunderstorms and earthquakes.

"Oh, that's right," he says. "I have to warn them."

Those last two words echo through the dream realm: *warn them, warn them, warn them.*

"Can I wake up now?" he asks.

One of the giants shifts. Maybe it leans closer, maybe it bends to get a better look at Al-Qaum in this place where he clearly doesn't belong. It moves its mouth, which seems to open and close and flap and shudder, to say, "No."

The word is like a sledgehammer.

"No?" Al-Qaum stands, or seems to stand, faces this impossible creature in this improbable place, and draws a weapon. He doesn't have a weapon, so he draws it from the sky, a kind of sword, something magical and mystical and otherworldly. "Did you tell me *no*?"

The creature smiles. When those lips stretch, the whole realm trembles. Thunder crackles. Why is there thunder? Why is there the sound of an ocean eating the shore? How long has he been sleeping, dreaming and drifting?

When he wakes, he doesn't know immediately where he is or why, but he knows he's clutching the hilt of a sword that shouldn't be here.

7.

Asteria stalks the creature. The drops of blood are like black splotches on black, but her eyes are accustomed to darkness in ways that her mother's aren't anymore. Hunting is her second nature. She tracks the creature through alleys, through glassless windows, through ruined walls and across unstable roofs. She moves like a thief, with agility and speed and stealth, with determination and intensity.

She finds the thing hiding in a cubbyhole, in a corner, back to the world, nursing its wound. The slice across the chest doesn't appear deep. It's just a creature, nearly mindless, autonomous but not malevolent. Asteria keeps her knife in her hands as though it's a talon, and it would be just as effective.

She asks, "Are you hungry?"

Startled, the thing turns, looks at her, hisses like a cat, and runs.

It can't get far. It's in a corner, and it has to get past Asteria to escape. It's cute, in a way, but it's a creature of the night, and its tail drips with the blood of her brother. She shows her blade before the creature can reach her. It flings itself back into the corner.

She sighs.

She returns her knife to its sheath.

The creature is hungry, most definitely, and also hurt—like Al-Qaum's, it's not a mortal wound—and it cowers in fear. To kill it now would be cruel. She's not cruel. "Don't make me regret this," she tells it.

Without bloodying her knife, she returns to the caravan to learn Al-Qaum has been sleeping in a room with a guard. The morning is nearly upon them. It's time to find their ship and brave the coming storm.

CHAPTER SIX

1.

Jack and his mother watch the ship approaching, the storm in its wake. Flashes of lightning highlight something in the clouds, a large winged thing like a demon, like an ancient god, like an impossible nightmare made real.

Either the crew of the ship don't see it, or it doesn't matter if they do. They race over the swells of the ocean, tossed and thrown by the water and the wind. Bolts of lightning rain from the sky.

"They're off course," his mother says.

The ship and its crew have been battered, beaten, devastated by whatever's behind them. Even if they are able to keep a course straight for the castle's pier, the storm will overtake them. They'll vanish behind that deluge into fog, mist, rain, cloud, storm surge, and monsters.

Jack doesn't know for certain they were aiming for the castle. That's a presumption, though it seems reasonable. He can see the sailors working, most of them sporting wounds of some sort, some more dead than alive.

Dead and alive are words that need new definitions in the other realms.

Jack looks down at the threads. There are several, strong, vibrant, both light and dark, leading straight over the ocean and into the storm. The winds don't affect them, but there's tension on those lines. They're intertwined in ways Jack doesn't like. One is so thoroughly crimson, a combination of blood and fire and blisters and raw exposed muscle. It's almost familiar.

The other is Lisa Sparrow.

He's sure of it.

He has to go into the storm.

"You don't, you know," his mother says.

"Of course I do."

She can't argue against that. Of course he does. It feels like years, but it's only been a few months since he met Lisa Sparrow. A chance meeting in a bar in downtown Orlando, a frantic rush of emotions, an imp sent to destroy him. His life changed that weekend, though it could have changed for the better.

Instead, it led him here, to the outer edge of another realm, staring into an abyss that moves toward him. The storm, as big as it is, is something alive, pulsating with the blood of its victims, and it camouflages something worse. It wants to consume him and his friends, but on this side of the castle wall he's in another realm. Safe. Relatively safe. He cannot stay on this side of the wall. He has to go forward.

He doesn't know if Lisa is in danger. He doesn't *need* to rescue her. He only wants to be reunited. The regular life she had made him dream of, the everyday nine-to-five mundanity of living, has been denied them; that doesn't mean they can't face whatever's next together.

But he *thinks* Lisa might be in danger. Too many people—creatures, powers, entities, gods—know of her because of the DarkWalker, and Jack Harlow isn't prepared to let her suffer because she once crossed paths with him.

To reach whatever realm is next, he needs that ship to take him there.

A light bursts to life on the edge of a pier. Like the beacon of a lighthouse, it shines out onto the ocean, it sweeps across the edges of the horizon, it highlights the amorphous texture of the approaching storm, and finally catches the ship in its beam.

In response, the crew doubles their effort. The captain shouts orders, but they're unnecessary. Everyone knows their role. The ship lurches toward the light. For a brief moment, it seems like they'll outpace the storm.

The storm, however, won't allow that. It increases in intensity. It extends its reach. It touches the ship's stern, obscures the poop deck and plucks sailors from it. The mizzenmast vanishes in the storm's haze. The mainmast seems to snap away, consumed by the storm.

"Hard to port!" the captain yells. Jack can't even see the captain. There's too much storm now. The ship is swallowed.

A strange silence follows.

Then the storm pitches forward, intent on the castle, on the border between realms, on the pier and everyone on it.

"You know them, don't you?" his mother asks. "They came with you."

"Are you ready to jump?" Jack asks.

"You know I can't."

"I can," Jack says. He grabs hold of his mother around the waist. She clings to him as he leaps out of the castle, through the hole he'd made, into a brief wash of the starlight above the castle, and into stormy weather.

The heart of the storm is like a wall, but its winds and rains reach far beyond that. They'll breach the boundary between realms. But had the storm been targeting the castle—or Jack Harlow?

He lands on the beach near the pier. The pier connects directly to the castle, which looms behind them like a wall between worlds, but it was too far to jump against those winds. It's a rough landing. He's more concerned with keeping his mother safe through the fall than protecting himself. His knees nearly buckle at impact. He makes a crater in the wet sand, and it's already half filled with rainwater and ocean.

"I'm okay," his mother says.

"Good. Another jump."

He doesn't give her a lot of time to prepare. This is

more horizontal, against the wind, so it's hard to judge. He lands on the pier, on long wooden slats threatening to come apart in the storm like sheets of paper. Behind him, nearer the castle, three shadows loom close. Ahead: the caravan, complete with the prisoner's wagon, are at the most extreme edge. They're over the ocean, surrounded by ocean, and shining a light so bright into the storm wall it's almost a sun.

At the last minute, before that wall reaches the pier, the ship bursts out of the mists, the captain yelling at the crew, its crew fighting to accomplish any little thing. They'll smash into and through the pier. The storm will be right behind them.

Jack rushes forward. His mother calls out to be careful, but there's no time for caution. He casts a psychic net about the ship to hold it in place, to protect it from the pier, its own momentum, and the fury behind it.

The storm blinds him. Rain and ocean spray pummel him. He nearly loses his footing as he runs, but the pier is long and wide as well as slick. The ship resists him. He's putting everything he's got into it, but the ship hadn't just been aimed in the direction of the pier, it had been propelled, as if shot from a cannon.

Anastasia's light redirects to keep the ship at its center. The storm crashes against them. The wind is horrible. The rain like bullets. The lightning constant and, now that he's in this realm, the thunder is relentless and deafening.

Anastasia's burning light, and the dark net Jack cast over the ship, slow it enough that when it hits the pier, nothing is shattered, and the troupe at the end of the pier aren't thrown clear.

The captain continues to shout commands, but the storm won't wait.

Without precautions, without care, the caravan throws itself onto the ship. It hasn't been tied, there's no plank, there's nothing really connecting it to the pier; and the storm rages against them. The horses seem to have been left behind, but not the wagon. They'd dragged it physically down the stairs and out onto the edge of the pier.

It's a pirate ship.

It's a wrecked pirate ship that probably shouldn't still be afloat.

The crew is half pirate, half East Indian Company, with maybe a few Pinkerton bounty hunters and ninja thrown in for good measure. Indeed, it's a motley crew, and not one of them isn't bleeding from any number of cuts, scrapes, scratches, and gaping wounds.

The caravanner climbs netting on the outside of the ship to reach the captain.

She reaches the deck, between the captain and his men, and starts issuing commands. "Stand down! Now! Don't make us erase your stories, untold, from this realm!"

The captain draws his saber. But he's unsteady on his feet, bleeding profusely from where a shard of wood still protrudes from his thigh—and another, less severely, from his forearm. He draws his saber, but can barely hold it upright. "I will die before allowing you to take my ship."

"Your ship is already taken," the caravanner tells him. "We may not outnumber you, but not a single one of your crew isn't already on the brink of death. We can *help*."

The storm attempts to suppress the words as she says them. Jack, watching from the pier, can barely hear them. Behind him, there are shadows, there are figures, there's his mother and others approaching the ship.

The storm, in its full fury, engulfs the pier.

2.

The storm strikes the pier, the ship, the people and shadows on or near the pier, the shore and beach, the castle walls, and Jack Harlow with all its fury.

It's like being in a blender. The pier, weakened by the crashing of the ocean and the pirate ship, in places shatters under the onslaught of the storm. The place where the caravan had been standing plummets immediately into the depths of a rising ocean.

The sky, a roiling amalgamation of grays before, is nothing but infinite threatening maelstroms, all the ends of insubstantial air worms with mouths made of black holes and other singularities.

Rain falls with such intensity, it splinters parts of the pier, and parts of the ship, and may shatter bones.

The thunder, on the inside of the storm wall, drowns out all other sounds. Layers of thunder boom and crash, while other thunders rumble and roil. It's a ceaseless, chaotic rhythm section made up of a thousand kinds of drums playing to spite each other.

The lightning is mostly invisible, lost in the murk, obscured by its own shadows, so that the flashes come through in weak and cracked colors. The bolts that are visible are close enough to singe the hairs on Jack's arms and neck.

The other side of the castle walls might be safe, being in another realm, but there's no place safe here. The storm is malignant and alive and hungry. And it's merely an emissary, a beginning of something, a bringer of ends of worlds.

Jack's still got enough watcher in him to see the past of this storm and storms like it. He was called the Destroyer of Hells, though in fact he only leveled one walled city in a single hell realm. This storm has devoured entire realities. Paradises and infernos.

Twilight realms. Earthlike realms without alignment. This storm is as old as any realm, a traveler between them, and when called upon—somehow, always by people unaware of what they're doing—it comes and consumes its fill.

But it is never full.

The storm is a raging beast of absolute and insatiable hunger. And it is driven forth by something stronger, something more substantial, something that leads with the storm and does all the real devouring. A creature massive in size, like a mountain under the waves, with massive gelatinous eyes on stalks, with tentacles like octopi and squid, capable of shifting its shape and changing its color. It's larger than the castle wall facing the ocean, larger than the boundary between realms, and it drives the storm beast before it—no, the storm beast is a part of it, like teeth that chew before swallowing the meat into the pit of acid that might be called a stomach.

When the octopus squid Lovecraftian Kraken thing is lit up by the lightning, it replaces the horizon, obscures the sky, looms over clouds and oceans. There's no attaching emotions or feelings to what it does. It's too alien. It's too much for Jack to understand.

But he's not alone.

His mother is beside him. She's a watcher, yes, so she should know things, and he knows the things she knows, but she shields herself from the storm and cannot see much.

There are the shadows, three of them, sisters, whom Jack should have recognized long before. They're maybe older than this leviathan, but all they can do is stare into this abyss.

And there's the king from the valley, the former king of Babylon, grinning, half naked, holding his arm out and his head up as if welcoming the embrace of the tempest.

On the boat, where the caravan troupe and the pirate ship crew work together to batten down the ship against the worst of the storm's assault, an impossible thing happens: the prisoner's wagon, trembling on the poop deck, cracks. The woods were special woods, and a dozen layers of magic on the outside held it together. Another dozen inside reinforced the wagon from any onslaught. The wagon cracks, and the sound is enough to make the thunder cower for a moment. Only a moment. The prisoner, insides, takes a deep inhalation. Even through the storm, Jack feels it.

Above the storm, above the clouds, over the body of the octopus squid Lovecraftian Kraken thing, another extraordinarily large creature sails on leathery wings.

Through it all, the thread connecting Jack to Lisa, on the other side of boundary to another realm, remains taut, and leads straight through the storm into the gullet of the Leviathan.

He grabs his mother and jumps onto the ship's deck. Others board more silently, more stealthily, more secretly.

He reaches the deck, the caravanner and the captain still facing off. He gets between them and shouts at the captain. "You have to drive us into the storm!"

"You're mad!"

They have to yell to be heard over the storm's fury.

Jack Harlow draws up on the captain, disregarding his saber and his wounds, and says, "You cannot outrun the storm. The only way out is into the heart of it."

"We'll all die!"

"Yes, we will," Jack Harlow says. All of us. Eventually. But not today."

The captain's eyes are bloodshot. He hasn't slept in days. He's been running full tilt since whatever mistake he made at sea. He's drunk nothing but rum and hasn't eaten a thing. Underneath the skin, innumerable diseases eat his insides. He's survived poison so many times, his blood is toxic. He's not afraid to die, but not anxious to do so. Yet, looking into Jack Harlow's eyes, in which all these secrets are revealed, he falters. He's faced sea creatures before—octopi, squid, Lovecraftian monsters, and Krakens—but never all of that wrapped into a single behemoth. He's beyond his wits, beyond his capacity, and beyond all semblance of reason.

He says, "Aye, you may be right."

And then the captain is shouting orders. The ship breaks free of the pier. It couldn't withstand the storm anyhow. They turn the ship around, aiming the mermaid on its bowsprit directly into the storm. It's not an easy trajectory. The force of the storm pushes it back. The crew works hard, but it's like a mouse trying to push against a brick wall. The storm rages. The ship rocks heavily. From elsewhere on the ship, Anastasia shines her light into the storm, into the face of the creature bearing down on them. So close to shore, it's mostly above the waves. It's like a sky itself, so mostly nothing else can be seen. Lightning skitters in nets around it. The light can't illuminate the whole of it at any one time. Its flesh is a rotten brown sheen. Its eyes are as big the ship itself. Its mouth opens, its teeth like stalagmites and stalactites around the opening of a cave. Ocean water rushes in and out of its mouth, over an impossibly black tongue. Maybe it thinks, maybe it doesn't, maybe it's merely driven by hunger, but it's also nasty, mean, wicked, evil, malevolent, and destructive, and it relishes all of this.

They sail the whole ship into its mouth. The captain brandishes his saber as though it might do something. Al-Qaum wields a weapon of his own, and shouts from an upper deck, side by side with one of the ship's crew who only remains standing because of momentum. The prisoner, at the back of the boat, breathes air from outside his prison for the first time in a thousand years. The Sisters of Shadow flock around Jack Harlow's mother, protecting her from the turbulent route of the ship. Over the tongue, then over the back of the throat like waterfall. The ship makes painful noises as they fall. Anastasia's light highlights the thick, bulbous inside walls of the esophagus.

The creature closes his mouth and swallows a city full of ocean water to chase the ship down its throat.

Jack Harlow holds the captain in one hand and the caravanner with the other as the ship goes vertical and plunges into unimaginable depths. They still hear the sounds of the storm, but now they're inside of it, at the center, protected from the worst of the wind and rain and lightning. Even the thunder is muted.

Ahead of them: a sea of acid and oversized anemone and urchins and sea dragons somehow surviving inside the creature.

But it's also another boundary between realms. The creature is itself another realm, like the fields on the other side of the castle, like the valley of the seers, like the desert surrounding Babylon. The inside of the creature is its own world, albeit one they would not survive long. The acidic seas already eat at the ship. Swordfish unlike any ever seen on earth leap through these sickly waters and brush against the sides of the ship. There are whales, giant whales, impossibly sized things that should not exist within the belly of another creature. Squid and octopi. The ghosts of fallen sailors, gnarled and translucent and distorted by the seas.

Through this, through the center of it all, toward what appears to be an island but is in fact another maelstrom. It tears the ship apart. Splinters the wood and cannons, shreds the sails, shatters the skeletons of half its crew.

The pirate ship, with its captain and the caravanner on deck, with Jack Harlow at its center, Anastasia at its bow, and the prisoner at its stern—with an enormity of power undefined and unexplored—sinks.

3.

Jack wakes on the shore of a beach. The sea behind him is filled with lava. Part of the ship sinks into that molten sea, while a thousand souls try to clamor onto the last pieces sticking up because, however brief, it would be a relief from the constant torment.

Across the shore, the caravan and the pirates and everyone else are scattered. The sands are red or orange and almost as hot as the lava.

Anastasia faces the prisoner. They must've both reawakened before Jack. He stares, but they're not moving. They're in each other's minds. Mother and son? Yes, but it's worse than that, yet they aren't fighting. Are they exchanging stories?

The blind king sits on the sand, picking at imaginary berries that should be growing near him. Alexis stares at the old man—through his blindfold, under which there are no eyes—in wonder.

Around him, half the crew is dead. The acrobat is dead. The pirates are mostly dead. The captain and the caravanner stand shakily on the unsteady ground.

There's no sun. They're in some kind of underground chamber, however immense it might be. Heat and light emanate from the walls, from fissures in the ground, from cracks in the rocks, from the molten sea and the river that feeds souls into it.

The souls are wisps of things, hardly substantial, whispers and memories of what they might once have been. Others hang from the ceiling, a thousand feet high, where red ants and red crickets and red spiders crawl across them. In the distance, the sound of screams echoes and echoes again, a ceaseless wave of screams undulating through the atmosphere.

"It's an inferno," the caravanner says, turning to look straight at Jack, angry and accusing. "You led us to hell."

"We knew you would come here," one of the Sisters of Shadows says. The middle sister, Corissa, the witness. Their voices aren't voices, but dig direct into his mind.

"One of the deepest, hottest hells," Lisette, the eldest of the sisters, says, grinning. "I've been waiting a long time for a true challenge."

Sibyl, the youngest sister, whom Jack has known longest, stands before him. She touches his cheek. There's tenderness there, and sorrow. A tear glimmers on her face, under her eye, though it's hard to say for certain any of the sisters have faces or eyes.

From somewhere far off, farther off than imaginable, there's a rumbling of thunder.

"I expected death inside the belly of the beast," the captain says. "I didn't expect this."

"But this is death," the blind king says. "Used to be, I would send my enemies here, to these shores, to burn forever in these flames. Look, there, on the surface of the sea: my enemies."

"There's a problem," Al-Qaum says, dragging himself through the sand and pointing with his sword—which defies description—at the prisoner.

The prisoner looks human, though his skin is gray like smoke. He and Anastasia circle each other, hands hanging open on either side of them, perhaps reviewing everything that's happened these past thousand years or more since he's been in her custody.

"There's another problem." Amelia Harlow, Jack's mother, stands further along the shoreline. The river of lava flows from somewhere. A road winds alongside it. On that road, marching toward them now, are legions of infernal soldiers, mutated creatures that maybe shouldn't be able to stand, armed with makeshift weapons, rusted spikes and silver spears and muskets older than the American Revolution.

"Ha!" the captain says. "And I thought we were ugly. Quick, can we salvage any of the cannons?"

His crew responds immediately, searching among the shattered ship.

Above, something like lightning races across the ceiling. It crackles, spills sparks, sizzles, and fries a dozen tiny creatures to a crisp.

Anastasia turns suddenly toward Jack. The prisoner turns, too, but with less enthusiasm. "There's another problem."

She's pregnant. She's been pregnant. But now she's bursting, she's ready to give birth. Her child—Jack's child—has in the past day or two fully gestated, and is ready to break free.

The prisoner grins. His teeth are crooked and splintered and the color of bruises. "The last time she was cut open from the inside, it was me." He seems gleeful at the idea of a sibling, something as strong as him, as powerful, as deep and painful.

Al-Qaum says, "I've heard no story to prophesize this."

Jack shakes his head. There's too much to process, too many people, too many loose ends, too many things beyond his control. He wipes sweat from his forehead, swings his gaze up and down the walls, realizes this is just one corner of this hell. It doesn't begin here, or end here, but it doesn't continue in any direction except through that approaching army.

He's dealt with hellish armies before.

He feels that strength within him again. He squeezes his fists, barely able to contain what's inside him.

"Do it," the king—or is he a jester?—says, laughing, rolling onto his back in the sand. "Burn the whole thing down!"

Sibyl, of the Sisters of Shadows, leans closer to Jack. She's ethereal, hardly a physical presence at all. Compared to the environment around them, her shadowy form is cool, almost cold, almost frosty. Without words, she says they're with him, they're with him to the end, they owe him for allowing her to escape the Shallow City, for reuniting the three sisters in death, for bringing them to this point where they can honestly feel the world around them.

Jack takes a breath. "Right," he says. It's not much, but when he releases that breath, it spills chillily from his lips. The cold drips onto the sand, absorbing and dissolving the heat of it. A few grains of red hot sand go gray, then shift to an arctic blue. A few grains at first, then a few more, slowly expanding. It'll take years to terraform an entire infernal realm. He'll need help of another sort to accomplish that.

The Sisters of Shadows are happy to help. They fade from this realm in search of other hells.

Jack, Jack Harlow, DarkWalker and Destroyer of Hells, has threads that tie him intricately to this specific infernal realm. He's never been here, but he's not alone here, he would never have been alone here, he might have spent several eternities suffering in this place.

He looks to the advancing army. Creatures that once might have been human walking on spikes that, with every step, drive again through their chests. Flesh peeled back, skeletons exposed, burning cinders growing in the place where once they might have had hearts or spleens or genitals.

Anastasia, driven by internal torments of her own, drops to her knees. The prisoner stretches a blanket under her—a blanket fashioned from molecules in the air.

The advancing legion, perhaps only on patrol before, suddenly charges forward, led by a lieutenant, a lower lieutenant, a kind of demon that might have evolved from the illicit union of pelicans and snakes.

"Go," the caravanner tells Jack. "We've got this."

The king still rolls in the sand laughing.

When Jack doesn't move, the caravanner rushes up to him, ripping the scarves from her face, and yells, "Why are we here?"

Jack shakes his head. "Lisa can't be here."

She slaps him. Hard. Hard enough that her hand leaves a mark that burns on his cheek. "Go get her."

He glances at Anastasia. He has a responsibility.

The caravanner grabs him by the face and squeezes tightly enough to crush his mouth into an O. "*We've got this.*"

"I can stop the army," Jack tells her.

"Look around," she tells him. "Who do you think we are?"

"She's right," the king says, popping up to his feet. "We're fucking *gods*." He reaches up with one hand, blindly, toward the ceiling. A burst of physical energy explodes from his arm, shooting straight into and through the walls of the realm, through a dozen tiny creatures, connecting him to whatever's beyond the boundary. Those creatures. He grins, straight at Jack, and yanks that piece of the ceiling down.

The ceiling, the sky, the upper boundary of the realm comes apart. Debris falls. A hundred insectoid hell-beasts slide down this extension of his arm. He opens his mouth so when they reach him, they flip like Hot Wheels over a ramp and down his throat. Then he turns toward the advancing army, these tortured soldiers who fight for the glory of a realm they would desperately not be a part of. He spits at them, from this great distance, launching hellish insects like cannons from his mouth. When they hit, they explode. The small explosions won't decimate an army, but every hit explodes one of the creatures into its component parts. Bits of flesh, mechanics, sticks, rocks, blood like lava, infernal flames that burn within them and keep them both sentient and mobile.

The prisoner, seeing this, laughs, and turns his attention to the advancing army.

The mother, lying on her back, screams with her contractions.

Jack realizes something then, something he maybe should have realized before. The king, the jester, whatever role he may be playing, is more than he appears. And the prisoner hasn't begun to extend the full breadth of his strengths. Even the mother, Anastasia—she was not always what she is now.

And they can, most definitely, withstand the might of an army, even an army from hell, even seven of them. Jack alone stood against seven, though that path—it was a path he'd already begun to travel—eventually led him here. To hell. A very real Hell, with a capital H, ruled over by a demonic king at its center.

They were far from that center.

So Jack ran.

Alone, but not truly, he doesn't have to hold back. He unleashes all his power, all his strength, all his speed. He runs from the shore and the ruins of the pirate ship. He runs along the path, and when necessary runs across the surface of the lava seas. His feet hit the flesh of souls, pushing them deeper into their torment. In the past, he wouldn't have cared. He knows now, though, that this will not be a permanent thing. There's been enough anguish, here and maybe in other hell realms, a persistent sociological structure invented and enforced by lesser beings.

He isn't a lesser being. He never was.

He runs miles this way, seeing little, following the path of his own connective threads that bind him and his lover, his perfect lover, his soulmate, Lisa Sparrow. She's at the center of this realm, bound in cuffs of fire, entwined by slithering silver coils, bleeding and crying, where she's been suffering for unknown eons.

Because time, especially within the infernal realms, isn't always consistent.

When he reaches Lisa Sparrow, she looks up at him. She smiles, briefly; his face is the first hint of relief she's had in untold ages. But the smile is short-lived. There's so much here she doesn't want Jack to see.

But Jack Harlow is a DarkWalker. All his life, before he was ever aware of it, he'd been able to see things in the dark that shouldn't be there. He saw into the hearts of mysteries. He didn't always understand what he saw, though there were times he thought he did. He didn't always learn from his visions, and he certainly didn't always do the right thing. Indeed, he'd done some horrible things along the way, and there's no escaping those facts.

But none of those things are worthy of *eternal* damnation.

These other realms have taught him one thing above all else: it doesn't end, none of it ends, you just keep going being the person you're pretending to be. Until the day you fully become who you are.

Maybe he's unleashed the full power of the DarkWalker before, but he's more than that. He's more than a label. Just as the label is more than him. He could have learned that seemingly years ago.

"Lisa!" he calls. She's encircled by more powerful demons, hellhounds, beasts, creatures, soldiers, abominations.

"Jack!"

It's the first words they've shared since she died, since the ghost of her began to fade from her apartment, since he slipped headfirst into the darkness. His head, for the first time possibly ever, is clear. He goes to release her, to cut the chains, to squash the flames. The legion around her doesn't like that, won't permit that. They respond with their full fury, turning every weapon— every blade, every curse, every flail, every spear and sword, every axe and pike and bladed fan and sickle and pick—every mace, every hammer, every trident—on Jack Harlow.

Then the demon himself, the lord of this realm, the massive behemoth that doesn't even have a name—a single horn protruding from his head like a dinosaur's, massive yellow eyes curved like a cat's, three fingers on its hands at the end of each of now four arms. He wasn't like that the first time Jack saw him on the streets of Orlando.

Seems like lifetimes ago.

The weapons pierce Jack's arms and legs and torso and chest. The legion of lieutenants lift him off his feet. He does what he can to keep his blood from spurting freely from him.

The demon looms closer, sweeps in, comes face to face with Jack Harlow. Its rancid breath burns with the heat of a thousand suns. "Finally," he says, his voice booming and echoing throughout the realm. "I've been needing to use your flesh, *DarkWalker*, to escape from this, my prison."

The legion of the damned cheer him.

He reaches forward. "You think you're strong," he says. "You were never strong enough." He lifts a silvery blade, which once upon a time belonged to Nick Hunter, and says, "This is the blade she hurt me with. Your *lover*." He says the word like a curse. "I've kept her here all these years, hurting her, tormenting her, as a means of pulling you to me."

He plunges the blade into Jack Harlow's chest. It's not what it once was, having spent part of its existence inside the body of the demon and so many years here in this internal place. It's taken on a life of its own, an infernal life, a hunger for things good. The other blades and pikes and spears hurt. This one, by itself, is agony. It burns through him, and cuts him more deeply than any of the others, more than physically, straight to his core.

The demon rips Jack free of the other blades and throws him bodily a hundred yards away. That knife still protrudes from him. And just like that, all the red around him, the blistering heat, the stench, fades to almost nothing.

Almost nothing.

Someone kneels beside him. Touches his cheek. Tenderly. He looks up. His vision wavers. "Naomi?"

"No," Naomi says. "Not just me."

Beside her and behind her: Kalinda, of Shangri La; the vampires Nick Hunter, Lady Chandra, and Jia Li; the Sisters of Shadows and an ice demon from another realm; Rana, the froglike dog creature with all those teeth; the spirit of the warlock Colton; Elizabeth Harlow, his sister; two Angels of Hell whose names he'd never known, whom he'd always thought of as Fangs and Scar; the bear Burke; the Raveness; the cat-like scavenger who had retrieved him from the lake under the Shallow City; even a few Ronin who had once been samurai and mystic ninja.

Jack Harlow takes a breath. A deep, thorough, refreshing breath of whatever magic Naomi has given him. She leans close and says, "We are not your cavalry,

Mr. Jack."

The demonic army rushes Jack's allies—Jack's friends. He doesn't know why they all stand with him, what they might risk or what they might gain. He only knows they came to help him in this, what must be his final confrontation, his final test, the final proof of his love for Lisa Sparrow.

With his own power, Jack Harlow pushes himself to his feet. He rips the knife from his chest. Blood flows freely from the wound. Let it. Let it scar him. Let him always remember this day.

He meets the demon's eyes.

"None of you should be here," the demon says. His voice carries weight and authority, especially in this realm. When he moves, the realm trembles. "I only want the *DarkWalker*."

He says it like a curse.

And he brings the DarkWalker to him.

Not Jack Harlow. Not at first. There are other DarkWalkers. There's the blind king. There's the prisoner. Anastasia had transformed herself into something else, but once upon a time, long before she ever came to Babylon, she had been a DarkWalker. And there's the *wælgeuga*, the old, old woman Jack had met under the Deep City, astride a dragon the size of cities—a DarkWalker itself who had broken into this realm through the hole the king had created. And there's Al-Qaum, leading the charge with the vorpal sword he stole from a dream realm. And Jack's daughter, Anastasia's daughter, born full-grown as a cross between DarkWalker and Light.

The demon, perhaps, could have defeated Jack Harlow, DarkWalker, Destroyer of Hells, despite all the lofty titles. The demon was a kind of DarkWalker himself, a progenitor of the first of them. The power that had ensnared him here was greater than any ever known on earth. But against the might of eight DarkWalkers—all of the DarkWalkers—every DarkWalker to ever walk the earth—the demon cannot withstand the assault.

He calls upon all the strength of his realm, but a frost spreads across it, a coolness exhaled by Jack Harlow.

He inhales the power of all his soldiers, his lieutenants and generals, here and in other lands. He takes into himself every suffering soul of his realm, the dead and the damned that had been continually arriving to suffer eternally. This builds him, physically, to be larger than his realm, like the octopus squid Lovecraftian Kraken thing, to be an infernal realm onto himself. But he also draws in that frost. It's inescapable. And he draws in things that have bled through the holes in his realm. And he finds a legion of beastly foot soldiers have been liquefied on a brief field of battle in one of his farthest corners.

The combined might of eight DarkWalkers beat him down, pummel him, restrain and defeat the demon. But it's Jack Harlow, with the knife Lisa Sparrow had once used to sacrifice herself battling this very same demon, who delivers the killing blow. The blade goes through the demon's heart. Not a metaphoric heart; there's no such thing to be found. Through its physical beating center, the core of it, its essence.

And it's Jack Harlow who tears open a breach in the fabric of this realm, doing so with a power he absorbed from blank pennies given to him by the Vaudoux—a god of mischief—so very long ago, and creates someplace new. Someplace that curls in on itself, like the realm into which the DarkCrawler had fallen. The whole of the realm goes in, and then the knife, before Jack seals it all within a single white crystal. The crystal doesn't glow. Instead, it absorbs light, and it absorbs itself, and it folds in on itself until there's nothing left of it or the demon.

What remains: a gray wasteland.

His friends remain. His allies. His new daughter, who will be a frightful power because of where and who she comes from. And Lisa Sparrow, still bleeding but no longer bound. She rushes to him. When they embrace and kiss, it's with the intensity a thousand galaxies across a thousand realms.

EPILOGUE

1.

A Foreman arrives. He's a stick figure with a clipboard. He looks at his board, then at Jack, then down at his board again. "I know you."

"Yeah."

"DarkWalker."

It's not a question, and it's no longer completely accurate, but Jack says, "Yeah."

"Right, then," the foreman says. "This is your realm. The plans are ready to be executed. With your go ahead, we'll begin."

"Plans?" Jack asks.

The stick figure shakes his stick figure head. "I'm just a working man here, Mr. DarkWalker. I'll do the job, but I ain't the one you ought to ask questions of."

"No, I suppose you're not."

"Leave it," Lisa says. "Let them build it."

The bulldozers and earth moving machines are already pouring into the realm.

"We recommend you and, er, your friends." The Foreman clears his throat. There are many of them, scattered over a fairly large area, some meeting others for the first and maybe last time. "Clear out. Make room. Construction waits for no one, not even the DarkWalker."

More than one head turns at that.

"For how long?" Jack asks.

"A standard day," the Foreman says.

There's a moment of uncertainty. Jack doesn't know what to do. Kalinda steps up, smiles, touches his shoulder. "We can escape to Shangri La for a while, if that pleases you."

"And when you get back," the Foreman says, looking through the paperwork, "it looks like lots of long sunrises over an ocean. It's rare, to replace a destroyed inferno with a twilight realm, but those are the orders."

2.

Because such concentrations of power are dangerous, because balance cannot possibly be maintained in such ways, the DarkWalkers go their separate ways. The *wælgeuga* and the dragon return to her self-made prison under the Deep City, where she can listen to her jazz records in peace.

The blind king returns to his place in the valley, at the request of the seers there, in part because they see better when he's there and in part because he sees better when they're near.

Al-Qaum tells Jack he'll go off to listen to more stories, and admits he may go searching for the source of his sword. It's a mystery to him, but he's pleased by mysteries.

The prisoner goes to wander. He wants a different story this time. He's had a thousand years to reflect on the things he's done, and maybe he can find a love of his own.

Anastasia and their daughter: she kisses Jack goodbye, and their daughter, who doesn't yet have a name, does the same. "I'll teach her as well as I can," Anastasia says. "In Babylon, of course, surrounded by the gray deserts, where she can unleash the full fury of her power and not hurt anyone."

"I don't intend to hurt anyone," his daughter says. "Not yet."

3.

After a week in Shangri La, celebrating with old friends, healing deep wounds, meeting people who have been involved from the beginning, Amelia Harlow says, "I will stay here, if I'm able."

"Of course you are," Kalinda tells her.

Jack and Lisa go together into his twilight realm. They arrive at the beginning of a long dusk. The sky stretches redly and wonderfully above him. Already, there are birds and butterflies and flowers and ocean breezes, and there's a small, unassuming hut on the edge of the beach where they can live, he and Lisa Sparrow. Here, they can learn about each other more fully, they can explore the corners of their private realm, and they can explore the depths of their love in their private personal happily ever after.

THAT CONCLUDES
THE ADVENTURES
OF JACK HARLOW,
DARKWALKER

SERIES DEDICATION

This journey started in the early 2000s
when Mery-et Lescher
called me a Night Walker.

Which obviously means something else.

The first book was meant to be
one and done.
It wasn't until years later,
before submitting it to EvilEye,
that I realized its potential
for so much more.

Mery-et Lescher did the original
cover art for the first four books
when they were published by
DarkFluidity.
She had intended
to do the last two books, too.
But time sometimes isn't a thing
you have as much of as you'd like.

The DarkWalker series
is dedicated to Mary "Mery-et" Lescher,
who was always supportive
of my wildest dreams,
and will be pleased to see
I was able to bring this one
to its conclusion.

NOTES AND ACKNOWLEDGMENTS

Thanks to everyone who read *DarkWalker*,
enjoyed it, reviewed it, criticized it,
and threw it across the room.
I promised this would get stranger.

Special thanks for the support of Mery-et Lescher.
None of these happen without you. I miss you.

Thanks to Paul Goblirsch, Kyle Lybeck,
and everyone at Thunderstorm Books.

Thanks to Rich Gorey,
who completed the art
for the covers of 5 and 6.

Thanks, also, to Brent Tiano,
to all my First Readers on all my projects;
the Five Horsemen (Mike, Mikey, Coop, Brian);
my various inspirations;
anyone who has ever taught me anything;
the ghost of Edgar Allan Poe;
my sister (and her husband),
in whose house I completed this work;
and my Mom.

And everyone
who hosted me on my travels.

I have missed people. I always do. I am so sorry.

And as always: Sabine and the Rose Fairy.

ABOUT THE AUTHOR

John Urbancik was born
on a small island in the northeast
United States called Manhattan
at the dawn of a terrible and terrific decade
and grew up primarily on Long Island,
but he has also lived in
Florida, Virginia, Australia, and Spain.
Currently, he is wandering across the United States.

His first novel, *Sins of Blood and Stone*,
came out in 2002.

The first *DarkWalker* novel
was originally published
in 2012 as the first of a series.
The rest of the series has remained hidden.
Until now.

John Urbancik also hosted a podcast, InkStains,
based on his writing project of the same name,
which led to his first nonfiction book:
InkStained: On Creativity, Writing, and Art.

www.DarkFluidity.com

Made in the USA
Columbia, SC
29 December 2020